About the Author

Annie Raser-Rowland was born in a snowstorm in Boulder, Colorado. After being raised in the baking summers of Fremantle, she spent two decades living in different parts of Australia making art, growing gardens, and travelling to countries where she could climb volcanoes as often as possible. She has recently moved back to Western Australia, where she is working on her sunburn, her backstroke, and how to think better thoughts about the Anthropocene.

Annie's non-fiction titles include *The Weed Forager's Handbook* and *The Art of Frugal Hedonism. Once* is her first work of fiction.

ONCE

ANNIE RASER-ROWLAND

Grattan Street Press

Contents

Acknowledgement of Country

Grattan Street Press, the teaching press of the University of Melbourne, acknowledges the Traditional Owners of the unceded land on which we work, learn and live: the Wurundjeri Woi-wurrung and Bunurong peoples (Burnley, Fishermans Bend, Parkville, Southbank and Werribee campuses), the Yorta Yorta Nation (Dookie and Shepparton campuses), and the Dja Dja Wurrung people (Creswick campus).

We also acknowledge and are grateful to the Traditional Owners, Elders and Knowledge Holders of all Indigenous nations and clans who have been instrumental in our reconciliation journey.

We pay respect to Elders past, present and future, and acknowledge the importance of Indigenous knowledge in the Academy. As a community of staff and students we are privileged to work and learn every day with Indigenous colleagues and partners.

Once

1257

It's too still in here to tell where it's coming from, but the smell of metal has been introduced into the air. The cave's usual smell is sedate and alkaline, made cosier by the pheromones and guano of two hundred broad-eared horseshoe bats. As the new smell sharpens, these bats begin to squabble, albeit drowsily. And the smell continues to grow.

If tourists transported back from seven hundred years in the future were visiting the cave, they'd pause while photographing the formation that might by then have been dubbed the Pink Elephant. Their nostrils would prickle with something flinty; their mouths would think about sucking pencil lead. But even as the smell bloomed into that of foul water emptied from a vase of chrysanthemums, the tourists wouldn't know that this wasn't normal. They would keep gazing at the Twin Towers, trying to decide if the obesely puddling pillars of hardened salts were mildly repulsive or breathtakingly beautiful. They won't ever decide, because they'll never come to this cave. This is for the simple reason that – in a few minutes – it won't exist.

A lather of grey-green froglets start to mess up the surface of the pond that has formed where monsoonal rains sheet off the cave's outer face.

'Glub, glub,' goes a fat bubble of methane as it is knocked from where it is trapped in the silt below the pond. The bubble belches to the surface and sends a water strider spinning.

Deeper beneath the pond, the fossilised vertebrae of a 1.4-million-year-old giant stork implodes, and the shockwaves kill thousands of microbes that live in the surrounding rock fissures. From an overhanging tree a long fruit drops, and a sunbaking turtle slips off her rock and into the water to take snapping bites out of the fruit as it bobs. The mealy red flesh is sweetly rotten in patches and full of grey popping seeds that remind the turtle of the eggs she is carrying.

They are almost ready to be laid, she thinks. The lid of the jungle above her is spitting birds now, vomiting so many pairings, colonies and flocks into the air that, as they cut in and out of the rainbow of themselves, they are startled to see how much of the sky they occupy.

A frantic skink slips like a tongue into a deep rock crevice, fleeing the suddenly searing air. Several dusky leaf monkeys slide down the bamboo they've been feeding on and canter downhill, ricocheting off each other like pinballs as they run. Other animals run too. So many thousands of them that this storyteller – who lives in an age where there aren't enough creatures left to let her imagine such a thronging – dares not attempt to narrate the gathering tangle of its form.

The earth's subcutaneous stuff roars towards the sun like a party popper. Superheated ash and gas ascend in a pistol-shot column into the upper atmosphere, up where nobody flies – not the bats from the cave, not the aeroplanes that will be invented and will smash their silver bodies into trillions of the insects those bats want to eat. The mountain is now like a face missing its jawbone, and its glowing gore runs in fat duvets over the jungle – over the tiny frogs and over the turtle, whose eggs are cooked instantly inside her. A *hundred* kinds of eggs are hard-boiled in their nests.

Galloping tides of burning rock, gas and ash incinerate entire valleys, then hurtle out onto the sea. They race on unchecked, boiling the water into a soup of dolphins and dropping instant-set rock castles onto the seabed as they sprint towards the next island. More animals curl and blacken: three-metre-long earthworms, slim yellow dogs with keen black eyes, slim brown people with mahogany eyes, cerulean kingfishers, lanternflies.

Up in the stratosphere, the sulphur dioxide gas shapeshifts into sulphuric acid and mingles with the ash. The brew fans its fingers over the globe like a fortune teller.

Part 1

Once Upon a Time

Once upon a time, the people of Europe do not have the foggiest idea that a volcano is erupting on the far side of the earth. They are splitting roofing shingles, trimming their hair on stools in the sunshine, arguing theology, peeling turnips – and they have more love handles than ever. They also have more pot bellies and more chins, on average, than at any time anyone can remember. No one wishes it otherwise.

For the past four hundred years, the world's currents have sloshed in such a way as to hug warm water around the North Atlantic lands. Above a cluster of lush, balmy islands that are yet to be claimed by the Portuguese (who will eventually cover the islands' slopes with a cloak of intentional dairy cattle and unintentional hydrangeas), an immense egg-shaped body of air has been forming particularly generous yolks, then wafting their yellow warmth to such distant places as Scotland, Denmark and Estonia.

The people of Europe have answered this warmth by moving up the mountains and stealing more farmland from the snow. Their grain has answered it by ripening faster and growing plumper heads. There have been more loaves on more tables, and more children have survived to have their own children more often than before the warmth. Just two weeks per year of extra sunshine has seen the Europeans fell so many trees to create new fields to feed all the new mouths, that a stork flying from Kenya to its breeding grounds in Poland looks down to see a mosaic of pale green inlaid with dark green – the inverse of what its grandfather ten times over had seen when flying the same route.

But now, a priest crosses the pine floor of the church in Small Medieval Village. (Let's call it SMV, for this storyteller lives in an age lousy with acronyms.) As the priest dips his quill to write the year '1296', the volcanic ash soup has ridden the stratospheric winds from a latitude of nine degrees south to fifty-three degrees north. It has draped a modesty veil of dun particles across the sky's bold, bright face, which has caused the temperature to drop. Frozen crystals slushing about in Arctic waters have taken heed and knitted themselves into sheets of ice. This new ice has reflected even *more* sunlight back into space, causing the temperature to drop further – and the ice to expand further. How cold all the new ice makes the passing ocean! How sluggish! With a heave-ho the current is tugged from a letter Z into a figure eight, and frigid water coursing beneath the toes of Iceland ceases to be sucked down an underwater cliff quadruple the height of Niagara Falls. Instead, it stays up near the ocean surface, circling the nearby landmasses like a glacial shark.

In the beech forests of Sweden, brown bears start digging their winter dens earlier. They line the floors with moss earlier, crawl inside with bellies full of blueberries earlier. In Norway, the very highest pastures are relinquished back to the trees, leaving the corncrakes fewer expanses of cropped grass suitable for strutting through whilst issuing their sharp, buzzing cries.

Brida

Once upon a time, Brida is sitting on a pile of bundled rushes in the back of a cart, bouncing. The man driving the cart never looks over his shoulder on the journey back from market, because he likes to drive the horse very fast as he fumes over all the poor bargains he has just struck, and to script everything clever he will say when next faced with that unimaginable array of scoundrels. Brida lies on her stomach, undoes her braids, and lets her hair blow out behind her. This weekly to-and-from market is the only journey she knows, and this is her first year of making it without kith or kin. She pulls the skirt of her kirtle up to get the wind buffeting her legs, then makes a droning noise into the pockets of green light between the rush bundles, carefully matching her sound to the movement of the wind. 'Clack, clack,' go the cart's wheels as they bump past a thicket of wild plum. In the bald, sunny hollow on the thicket's south-facing side, an adder is coiled in perfect slumber, its digestive juices lovingly extracting nutrients from a bank vole it caught three days ago.

The first sniff of smoke from SMV sees Brida sitting up reassembled, and she climbs down by her family's cottage with her market coins clinking – though not so many this week, as the new axe head cost some of what the eggs and rushes got her. She and the cart driver roll the unsold rush cylinders onto the ground, both as silent as each other while the horse sweeps its nose hopefully across the hardened earth. The driver swings himself up onto his seat, becoming a silhouette against the cobalt sky, and off he clops.

When Brida enters the cottage, she finds her mother dead in the hearth room.

The baby that had been making half-inch fists in the woman's uterus that morning is lying next to her, bluish and streaked with hardening greasy curds.

Orban / The Father

Eight months earlier, Brida's father Orban had gone to the well at dusk and met a traveller from Flanders with whom he'd sat talking all evening. Orban was sharp as a toothpick, and his awareness of his own under-exercised wit and capability made him morose and ecstatic by turns. He wove, working on his cousin's loom in his cousin's rooms, on a street crowded with textiles workshops, in the town nearest to SMV. In the work-shop's rafters, small grey spiders wove grand sails, undeterred by the flying fibres of wool and flax that rapidly furred their creations' lower reaches.

In the final months of Orban's apprenticeship, his sweet-heart's belly had begun to swell. The cousin had sanctioned a marriage between the two, but with evident displeasure at this insult to the terms of the young man's bondage. Ten years later and he still chivvied Orban about the misstep, still found reasons not to let the woman join his household. So Orban continued to sleep alone on a pallet by the looms – but for the Sabbath and other holy days, and also those winter weeks when the weather became too harsh for leaving the shutters open to light the looms. Then he'd stride the eight kilometres back to SMV and hold his wife, altogether forgetting that he had a daughter until he'd soaked up enough softness to settle his frustrations.

That traveller from Flanders had worn an embroidered purse and had shining pinheads of sweat on his upper lip. He'd poured a bucket of well water over his dark red hair and told Orban about how weavers in his hometown of Lille were richer than nobles these days. How the centuries of warmer weather had dried out the Flemish marshes enough that the remaining water could be neatly drained into dykes. And how the land between the dykes had turned out to be incomparable for raising sheep. The sheep that grazed there had been found to grow incomparable wool, and the local weavers had been able to perfect their craft and ask incomparable prices for their cloth. The cranes – who'd once stalked frogs across the wide sodden lands knowing themselves to be the tallest creatures there – now chased minnows along the dykes and looked up at the ankles of sheep.

Orban, the traveller from Flanders didn't say half of this to you, and yet still you became a man possessed. By the end of the month, you'd taken your aptitudes and your flying fingers and headed west. You promised to return with such skills that the guildmasters would beg you to finally accept the title Master Weaver – and with it, their permission to establish a workshop of your own.

Brida

Brida runs blindly to the midwife's cottage, and they both jog back through the sunset, the midwife not pausing as she yells a neighbour out of her house to join them. The grown women's flapping veils are red as rosehips in the sinking light. Brida's tiny, cold brother is baptised by the midwife, who then announces him to have died just as she'd finished speaking the sacred words. There are no similar kindly lies for Brida's mother.

It's a village, so both the women know full well that there's been no message from Orban in the months since he left. His two brothers will get back to the family cottage from the fields soon enough, but the midwife wants Brida to come wait for them at her house, where she has a barrowful of cabbages to finish cleaning the slugs and beetles from.

The girl won't go with her because she feels that the top of her head is erupting – slowly, like a molehill forming. She throws pieces of firewood at the women until they leave. Then she throws more at the chickens who are hanging about wanting to be let in somewhere safe for the night. The distraught birds scatter down the hillside and find branches above the river to roost in. A pullet will die of cold before the morning.

✕　✕　✕

In that vacuum between witching hour and sunrise, Brida lies on her straw and listens to the sound of her two uncles snoring across the hearth. Up and down, up and down, like a long wind bending and releasing the wheat. Yesterday at last light, these brothers of her father had dropped their sickles and sat down between the newly stubbled furlongs with every inhabitant of SMV who wasn't lame, ballooned with pregnancy, or gone to do market business. Silently at first, everyone had torn chunks of rough bread with hands still so engorged with work that it was difficult to bend their fingers. They'd swallowed golden ale so thirstily it was as though they aimed to complete a gilding only partially accomplished by the simmering golden sun and the blinding golden wheat. After too little time, the women had slapped the crumbs from their hands, collected their gleaning baskets, and returned to the village with the children to feed animals and hearth fires. The men had lain and drunk more ale and thought separate and overlapping thoughts. Cats had seen that there were no heads on the wheat now to block their view, and had trotted sharply into the field to hunt the mice who were splitting between their incisors those fallen grains that the women had missed.

When Brida's uncles had discovered the corpse of their sister-in-law, drunken tears had oozed down the grimy gold of their young faces. Then people had come and gone from the cottage late into the night while Brida feigned sleep and watched through the gable of her elbow. She'd seen a large moth fly through the doorway behind the priest and bang into the same wall where a dormouse had lately made a tunnel. She'd felt herself begin to menstruate – only her second month now, so she'd had to put her fingers between her legs to check. She'd smelled the moment when the late summer's heat finally left the earth alone to emit its damp. She'd watched the older uncle's wife – who won't speak to him anymore and has gone back to live in her own family's cottage – draw her cheeks back like a horse new to the bit as she looked at the broad bloodstain that Brida's mother's haemorrhage has left on the floor.

Now, the threads of light that slip past the window shutters shiver in the dawn wind. Brida pinches one near her face with her fingertips and thinks about how things will be. Starting today, she will have to tend to both her uncles alone – at least until the younger marries, and he is a man who jeers at women to hide his fear of them. When Orban returns, she'll be servant to all three until he takes a new wife. Or until Brida becomes one herself.

The space beside the girl where her mother's large, warm body should be suddenly seems like a chilly weight that will crush her if she doesn't escape it, and she quickly stands and pulls on her surcoat, then slips her comb into its pocket. She squats by the hearth and uses three fingers to scoop big dollops of pottage into her mouth, not wanting to clink the ladle against the side of the three-legged pot.

Brida has looked at this pot every day since first opening her eyes while her mother breastfed her beside it – but she's still too young to pause at the idea of never seeing it again.

Above the river, the chickens are shitting their waking shits into the water, and aquatic beetles trundle-swim out of the silt to gobble the nutritious clots as they dissolve downwards. In the cottage, the girl takes her drop spindle and wraps it in her good apron. Then she thinks of the axe head, and she rolls that into the bundle too.

Quietly now, Brida! Push that door open with cunning muscles, and do not let it clunk behind you in the new day's breeze.

Rocks

Once upon a time, bits of leaves, twigs and dead insects' bodies blow into seams in the hardened lava and decay there. Monsoonal downpours collect dust and scour granules from the pillowy rock, adding minerals to the pockets of organic matter. A Christmas-grass seed blows into a moist crevice and sprouts. A pink-headed fruit dove craps into a rock pocket, and a *Lansium* tree germinates from its droppings. These things happen again, and again, and again.

Where tephra covers the land like a vast Georges Braque painting, it is mingled with the confetti of every plant it blasted past. Scraps of bulb and tuber sniff the light that strobes the rain-darkened days, then send shoots up to test it. Their roots begin to crosshatch the spaces between the rocks, and the crosshatchings become new sites for soil. Lizards discover the buffet of exposed rock and stay to draw its heat into their blood. Perched atop vertices that once met deep in the heart of the mountain – before it turned itself inside out – these lizards flick their tongues to taste the sky. They start families, and the humus becomes richer with each generation of their corpses.

In some places the island is buried beneath a hundred metres of pumice. This pumice sheds mainly silica, and the resulting glassy soils invite mostly the fronds and fishbones of ferns. When the ferns sporulate, they float the pumice fields with rusty orange spore clouds, and the protein in those spores attracts parrot finches, chattering lories and three kinds of mouse. These are pursued by hawk-eagles, scops owls and goshawks.

Everyone's faeces and fallen bodily fragments build a layer cake with the pumice particles. A *ficus* takes root.

Brida

Brida's head feels like a cracked egg that is leaking albumen. The woods flounce about her in the gusty morning like overgrown mastiff puppies, and she barely knows how to think the question, *where will I go*, because it's never been a choice before.

As she leaves the coppiced willows of the river flats and heads into taller forest, some trees are already pulling the chlorophyll out of their foliage, making visible the red and yellow pigments left behind – like understudies finally stepping out of the chorus into starring roles. There is no texture of ground here that Brida doesn't know: moss journeying along ridges of protruding root and over bulging stones; fibrous yellowish mats of wilted bulb foliage; rotting leaves that – if you scrape down to where the soil rushes up to greet their bottom layer – release tiny circuses of springtails.

She passes two traps that she'd watched her uncles set earlier in the week, finding both sprung but empty. Several autumns ago, the brothers had trapped a badger near here – a big enough creature to be a poaching offence. They had emptied the firewood basket, put the badger in it, and laid some wood on top to cover the curled, wire-furred body. They'd caught her following them that day, and the younger uncle had shaken her so violently that her jaw slammed open and shut until one of her baby teeth, just loose, had leapt out of her mouth towards him.

Now, she resets the traps just as she has seen him do it, performing the act as part payment for the axe head. Seven female mosquitoes take advantage of the quivering concentration of her hands to siphon up some blood, and their bodies begin converting it into the amino acids needed to make the yolk protein in their eggs.

Brida forages like a boat hauling in an anchor. Her long, hard mouth opens again and again for dewberries, blackberries, hazelnuts, dandelion flowers, watercress, damsons that have half-dried on the tree, orpine and chickweed. A thrush breaks into song. The forest becomes resinous and starts to topple down an impossible slope. To steady her descent, Brida goes crabwise, hooking her fingers around the cold white-quartz outcrops that glitter from the gloomy sponge of fallen needles.

Far below, by the thrumming river, an otter deposits a spraint full of pike bones onto a shelf of fibrous roots, then transforms into poured mercury as it re-enters the water.

The slope peels around a bend and softens. The girl starts to pluck mushrooms as she moves. She takes off her surcoat, folds it to make a pouch, and organises the fungus inside it as smoothly as silk handkerchiefs laid in a duke's dresser – these can be her capital when she reaches wherever she's going. She gives her yeasty fingertips a sniff.

The forest staggers up and down here amidst great cubes of broken rock, and is frequently interrupted by gullies that trickle with streams made docile by the long dry summer. Then there comes a roaring noise that builds steadily until she reaches the series of wide, low waterfalls that are generating it. Brida crosses them by way of a great fallen yew amidst the spray, and the air seems to continue effervescing about her even after she reaches the far side.

Up a tangled incline she huffs and puffs and is rewarded by a generous unkinking of the ground. The trees thin and begin giving way to brambly clearings, which hop with the whirring and clicking of winged insects. At the edge of one of these clearings, water is seeping from between two slabs of rock, greening everything in its path. Brida follows it down to where it lies in wide mirrored discs framed by squelchy moss. When she drinks, water invades her nostrils and sheets down her chin, and something difficult gets washed away. Two years ago, Arnest – her younger brother by only eleven months – had still been alive, and they'd found this place together. It had been February, and the pools had had thin lids of ice on them that they'd lifted off in shards and used to make a glass barn.

On the south side of the clearing, there are five ash saplings that cling to the skirts of the weeping rock. There's a point where rock gathers momentum and becomes a stubby cliff. There's a muddle of fallen trunks under a collapsed section of the cliff. And at the base of the highest point in the cliff, there's the opening to a small cave. Brida ducks inside it and squints around herself. Her breath is moving in a short, steady loop now. She unrolls the axe head from her bundle, places it on a ledge, and covers it with a layer of rubble.

This storyteller is becoming aware that she should describe how Brida's long, narrow wrists have freckles dusted over their topsides like flour over a loaf. How her nose has a sharp bump in it like her father's nose has, and how her hands are as exquisitely adept with a spindle as his are at a loom. How, like the well water in SMV, she has an alkaline nature and how, like the sky above SMV, she sometimes has a moist, looming presence that provokes tempers. How she asks many questions but often looks irritated by their answers. How sometimes when a wealthy cleric passes through the village, she gets stuck for days afterwards trying to map the differences between them.

Part 2

Once Upon a Time

Once upon a time, the sky is epic. A young stork stands within this sky, atop the city wall, zipping its feathers together. Below the stork stretch three lines that are familiar to it: the line of the wall, running beneath the bird's long black feet; the line of the stream outside the wall; and the line of the road, which heads towards the city gates and is the congealing of all the smaller roads coming from places with smaller numbers of people living in them. There is warmth in the stones of the wall yet, which means there is time yet to build wing muscle sturdy enough to get to Africa on.

By the stream, tanners scrape connective tissue from hides, and shreds of it wash down onto the bank and wrap themselves around the bases of the reeds. On the road, a woman's veil blows off, and a man leaning against a stationary cart eating a hard-boiled egg retrieves it for her. (The stork watches but doesn't recognise the egg as being something like what it came from.) Far, far up the line of the road, a girl is extracting a pair of shoes from the bundle under her arm and pushing her feet into them. It is Brida. The stork glides down to a wet spot in a field where cattle have pugged up the mud into miniature ponds, and begins scanning them for tadpoles.

This pipsqueak of a city is twenty-six kilometres from SMV, and Brida has chosen it because she is attempting to pull a draw-bridge of distance and crunkled terrain up behind herself. This storyteller can reveal now that Brida will stay here for two-and-three-quarter years, and in that time will see only three souls known to her: the SMV bailiff with the caterpillar eyebrows, a large roan gelding that had belonged to the smith in that village, and her father.

When she spots her father, her chest rolls back on itself like the neck of a stork about to utter its clacking sound. He is wearing hose that have been dyed stork-leg red, and his soft leather boots have folded cuffs with a scalloped edge. He sings something in a comic falsetto as he turns back into the doorway of the house he'd been standing by, and the laughter of several men erupts. The sound is soft, red, and scallop-edged in the dreary afternoon.

Brida

HERE ARE THREE vats of aged piss arranged in the sunshine, and here are Brida and two other women standing in the nostril-pricking liquid and stomping on newly woven cloth. 'Slosh, slosh,' goes the cloth as they work it beneath their feet to meld its fibres. The cold urine clouds, then becomes opaque as the ammonia in it strips the lanolin from the wool. When one of the women bends to turn her cloth, she can see midday's towering cumulonimbus reflected around her bare calves.

With these two women and their kin, Brida sleeps in what had once been a fashionable townhouse but is now a rotting, splintering shape with a charred roof. In her first month in that house – let's call it Rotting Splintering – Brida dreams of a giant white snake that swims in a brown river. For a long time, it undulates against the bend of the river, blurred by the silty water, then drops silently down into the obscuring murk.

In her third month in the house, she sits cross-legged on the floor with the head of a woman three times her age resting in her lap, stroking it as it rocks against her thigh with jerking sobs. There is nowhere Brida would rather be in that moment, and when the crying finally stops, she sings the head a hymn in her low voice and tucks some escaped greying hairs back under the woman's linen veil.

Afterwards, all the snot and tears have left a salt-rimmed shape like a beard on the wool of her kirtle.

In her eighth month in Rotting Splintering, Brida follows her father from the house where she first saw him to another, where the open shutter shows him crossing the room to kiss a calm-eyed woman. The woman is dipping rushes into melted tallow while using her foot to rock a florid baby in a low cradle.

On her way back to Rotting Splintering, Brida looks over her shoulder as she mounts the crest of a sloping street. Over the city walls she can see the long line of the land on the far side of the valley, where big pale cliffs break free of the forest.

In her tenth month, she steals a needle. Also a date, which is the most delicious thing she has ever tasted. She learns a new braid from the girl who brings the milk.

⨯　⨯　⨯

It's her thirteenth month of living in the city when Brida begins leaving its boundaries to gather mushrooms. Everyone in the house tells her that she has a blessed eye to always come back with such a pile. One of the couples sometimes talk between themselves about how she shouldn't go about alone so much as she does. But they say nothing, having other, closer people to worry over.

In her twentieth month, she goes to mass and gazes at a picture of a ship scratched deeply into the wooden pew in front of her. 'How *big* is a ship?' she asks the husband of the woman who'd cried into her lap, and he talks at length about one he'd seen catch ablaze in the Bay of Biscay, its decks drenched in spilled whale oil, the men diving from it into the sea like plummeting gannets.

In her twenty-ninth month of living in that precarious house, Brida ventures onto a frozen wetland. She clutches often at handfuls of the great tasselled rush that is busy dying back in dark clumps all around her, but still she slithers in her treadless boots. Somewhere below her a muskrat is tugging hanks of aquatic plant out from beneath the ice.

She's approaching the far side, hoping to find bittercress there, when a figure – a small, youngish man with cheeks drawn into rose blotches by the cold – hurtles out of the thickets of downy birch. A wild boar appears, galloping after him. The man skids on the slushy mud and careens headlong onto the ice, reaching towards Brida as if for salvation. The boar has halted where the mudbank does, and steam is pouring off its heaving torso. Brida grabs at a stand of rushes and hauls herself sideways out of the flying man's path, but before he reaches the spot where she'd been standing, he slips and pitches forward. A jagged branch sticking out of the ice rams into his throat when he falls. Immediately, the spread of hot blood starts melting the frozen wetland under his shoulders – which sink slowly downwards while his neck stays angled up because of being stuck through.

The boar turns back into the birch to continue his search for sows in oestrus, while beneath the ice the muskrat is headed towards its breathing hole, its fur decorated with tiny air bubbles like bright silver beads.

Brida slides her way to an island of vegetation. She rips down an armful of spindly growth, then lays it alongside the body to balance on. Parts of her are juddering uncontrollably. She rotates the dead man's belt pouch around his narrow hip bones and extracts some coins, a flint and steel, and a knife that's slung beside the pouch. After a pause where the blood in her own unscathed neck begins to feel like a tongue that has turned the wrong way around, she fetches a rock.

Then Brida, you knock the branch out of the man's throat so that you can pull his clothes off over his head, and you tilt his body into the hole that his blood has burnt in the ice.

✕ ✕ ✕

Now she dreams about the oldest coppiced oak in the woods by SMV. The stump that it gets chopped back to twice a century is over five metres wide. She figures out that if you lie on the stump and tense your feet in a special way, the wood turns into a kind of golden paint, and you sink into it. When you step out, you're basted in a warm, burnished coating that takes days to fade. She wakes up feeling very smooth – and even more separate from the people she's placed herself amongst.

In her thirty-third month in Rotting Splintering, Brida brings home a fat eel that she sees writhe out of a sackful of them being pulled into the monastery in a barrow. 'Thwk, thwk,' goes the eel's dark length against the ground as Brida darts across the street to grab the half-dead creature. She imagines the satisfied face her mother would have made upon receiving it. But at the house, one of the husbands says this to her: 'You have but by one hair taken meat from the mouth of God, and with enough eyes about to watch you do it too. The blow of the law may come down upon us all – and double, for having kept you when you are runaway. You've brought the stain of sin to our house, and I would see you step out of the door and not return, for you have threaded me with a nervous humour.'

Over the days that follow, the man's wife reminds him of Brida's canny handling of the geese, her valuable deftness with yarn, their Christian duty to teach her better ways than did those who raised her. But his discomfort inflates rather than abates. He makes his mind up to report the girl, and is bitter at himself for not having done it when she first showed up.

Brida slips out of Rotting Splintering like an eel slipping from a poorly tied sack. It is March, and the storks are on their way back from Africa.

Growth

ONCE UPON A time, it is raining on the ex-volcano.

When rain falls on fresh volcanic tephra, it can release leachates of fluorine, chlorine and sulphur compounds, poisoning the surrounding vegetation for the creatures who eat it. Monsoon after monsoon has finally flushed these leachates away, and animals from stick insects to muntjac deer are chomping upon the sea of glossy leaves that have crowded into the acres of gargantuan rubble.

Where pumice dominates, the growth is less exuberant. The grass that sprouts in this pumice soil can't find enough cobalt, and it says to the mouths of the long-horned cows that graze on it, 'I can't give you what you need.' The cows graze all the same, and some develop shattering spasms that eventually wear them down to bones, and then they lie down and can't get up again. The grass tuts as it takes their bodies into its body, and next season it comes up stronger, grows taller, feeds the cows better.

Throughout the world, the trunks of five trillion trees continue to thicken with growth. In seventy years' time, two of them will be chopped down for a monastery that is enlarging its tithe barn. The monks have God's coffers at their disposal, and the new oak beams are well-footed and protected by generous eaves; they will still be standing in seven hundred years' time.

That's when dendroclimatologists will take a sample from one of the beams. They will measure the widths of the annual growth rings, the density of the wood laid down at the end of the growing season, and the amount of carbon-14 present in each ring. They will note how the rings get skinnier and skinnier with each decade that passed after the volcanic pea soup dampened the sun.

Brida

There you are on the road again, Brida, gaze like a freshly sharpened pencil beneath the brim of your felt hat. Also below the hat are the stumps of your braids, sawn off with the knife you took from the man your brain has dubbed 'the pigman'. On your body are the pigman's linens, tunic and breeches, and on your feet are his shoes, their toes stuffed with grass to make them fit. In the long conical basket on your back is the pigman's winter cape, the squirrel fur around its neck still stiff with his blood. Of course, the hat is the pigman's too, and the belt from which hangs his knife and pouch. You imagine their weight at your waist to be a cock and balls, and you use the feeling to help you walk wide like men do.

The landscape is pulsing with seasonal anticipation. Violets lie in pert carpets and waft their delicate scent towards butterflies. Plush catkins appear on male goat willows, and an even plusher wildcat sharpens his claws on one of their trunks, then deposits a turd that is elegantly packed with all the indigestible bits of a mole. Raven couples patrol the airspace above nests that they have carefully lined with moss, hair and strips of bark. Woodpeckers – great, middle and lesser-spotted; green, three-toed and white-backed – hammer nursery holes into oak, poplar, apple and beech. Their skulls contain special spongy bones that help to absorb the shock of each strike, and their brains are egg-shaped so as to present a more generous surface towards the incoming force. The planet's skewiff spin lures the sun higher into the sky, and the sun lures the slow worm out to bask.

When the ground warms up, Brida takes off the pigman's shoes to save their leather and adds them to the backpack-basket. Beneath its straps there are fresh slicks of sweat in each armpit. This sweat clangs with fear chemicals, and the smell of it forms a question mark for Brida above her decision to leave the town. Her head fills with gravy if she tries to answer this question, but the soles of her feet are winter-soft, and the work of zigzagging from one friendly surface to the next soon becomes absorbing enough to thin her thoughts from a stew into a watery gruel.

She wends through fen and fern, wades through three dabbling streams and a racing river, and pushes through a sea of whippy ash seedlings that have colonised an abandoned field. She stops and feels every nerve ending in the soles of her feet thundering information up to her cerebral cortex. She is standing in front of the parent tree to all the saplings. Its twigs, still nude of leaves, are erupting with black buds like tiny hooves. Seven of its flung-out arms are balancing storks' nests, much as a plate spinner balances plates. These nests are made of roots, sticks and grasses, and they are wider than Brida is tall. Some of them are taller than Brida is tall too, their creators having returned to mend and extend them year after year.

Despite its girth, the tree is oddly dwarfish and sprawling for an ash. A mild cleft runs down the length of its trunk. When it was a sapling, it had been split vertically by a man from a nearby village, then two other men had held the halves of the young tree apart while the first man pushed wedges into the bottom of the split to keep it open. Three children, each with an arm or leg that luck had mangled or palsied, had been encouraged forward from the waiting crowd. Each child had been undressed and helped to step through the 'V' in the ash, and when they were done, the tree's wound had been smeared with loam and bound back together with wrappings.

As the light begins to dwindle, up into this tree Brida clambers, and out along one of the fissured limbs. She crawls into a nest and pulls on all of her extra clothes. As she falls asleep she hears a barn owl's wings softly shuffling the air between her and the stars like a deck of cards.

Cave

Once upon a time, a jay is unearthing an acorn it cached last autumn.

Brida is sitting not far off, perched on a fallen branch near the mouth of a cave. It's the cave where she left the axe head.

The girl's eyes are like electrons pinging around the clearing. They are bouncing off each beetle, each wisp of fur that has stuck to the fuzzy edge of a mullein leaf as a creature passes. This place is confiding to her that people don't come here. She feels how the ground is not trodden upon, the foliage not moved through, by humans seeking all the things that forests have to give. The feeling slides into her fascia and her nervous system, and a hundred thousand tiny locks inside her click open.

She eats the second-to-last piece of sausage in her basket, then sets five deadfall traps. She eats a hunk of the loaf she has bought with one of the pigman's coins, then digs a hollow in the earth. She heats stones in a fire, puts them into the bark-lined depression with some water, and simmers a mass of nettles into stingless surrender. She eats nettles. Then she digs out three of the pondlets beneath the weeping rock so that they connect and deepen into a bigger pond. She has halted the water in its slow tracks down the flank of the glade.

Each time she stops to eat she tries to decide where to go, but the thoughts feel like cumbersome intruders, and she busies her kinetic self with harvesting a pile of green bracken to sleep on. The weather – as is its wont – changes, and a suddenly grizzled sky is dropping a gust of warm raindrops onto Brida's freckled brow. The drops are as big as tadpoles, and she takes off her hat so that she can feel them hit the part in her hair.

Part 3

Once Upon a Time

TAKE ALL THE new ice that the oceans have birthed since the egg that became Brida was fertilised by the sperm that also became Brida. Cut it into tiny discs and sew them together with fishing line, and it would make sequinned dresses for x thousand narwhals. Chop it into cubes the size of dice, and it would fill every glass of diet cola that will ever be poured in every one of Alaska's future ski resorts, x million times over.

In this future of ski resorts and cola, some scientists on Baffin Island in the Canadian Arctic will perform tests on the roots of some dead plants – roots that will have been revealed, intact, by receding ice. The scientists will find that the plants died by being entombed in this ice when it formed sometime around the turn of the thirteenth century. This storyteller will read about their findings in an online journal.

1317

It's 1317, AND it's springtime in SMV! Seven hundred years from now, people who have never farmed (which will be most people) will have a vague notion that spring is a season of plenty. They will generalise nature's having unfurled her fist to reveal such jewels as flowers and birdsong to include calorific bounty – rather than merely its promise. They won't heed the difference between the neon green of an apple tree's first leap into leaf and the worn verdure of its canopy when its fruits are rich balls of water and sugar in late summer. They won't distinguish between the voices of birds trying to get laid, and the voices of birds defending hatchlings in their nests.

But the residents of SMV know differently – as do all residents of temperate climates in 1317. Spring is the hungriest time. And *this* spring is the hungriest that anyone can remember.

A cottage by the forest smokes enthusiastically. Its smoke paints empty stomachs on the fair blue sky, and inside the house there is no ham, no rabbit, no hedgehog hung above the hearth fire to catch the smoke on its way out. There is an impressive oak trestle table, a good stack of slim ash poles ready to be worked into tool handles, and a fine beechwood grain ark with next to no grain in it. A woman scoops a handful of kernels into a pot and then heaves air into her pinched lungs as she replaces the ark's lid. She sighs this way because she is starving, and her body doesn't have enough iron in it to send oxygen to where it's needed. And she sighs this way because her children are starving too, and she doesn't know how she's going to keep them alive. Her teeth are becoming peggeldy-loose in her gums.

Outside the cottage a five-year-old boy lies along the back of a stocky black horse, soaking up the weak sunshine. An eight-year-old girl sits on a log and picks through a pot of dried peas, pulling out the mouldy ones and chucking them to the brown chickens that scratch about her feet.

It is a bonny house, a bonny sky, a bonny scene.

The boy's face glitters and opens and closes its doors like a Fabergé egg. His eyes are tracing the paths of the small blue butterflies that prance through the air around his perfect skull. There is something loose about those eyes when the glitter departs; maybe his brain is damaged or has a different blueprint from most brains. Everyone in the family knows by now that it is more work to keep him to a task than is saved by his doing it. Words – be they ones of admonishment or praise – seem to hop about him like frogs, only registering if they land plumb in his lap or if he spots one he particularly likes.

The girl's wiry shoulders peck at the fabric of her kirtle as her hands work. Inside her skeleton she suddenly feels the sap of her supple youth surge, and she springs to her feet and hauls her brother down from the horse by one of his ankles. She catches him in the noose of her arms and cries, 'Herr Hans, Herr Hans! Show me your palms!' This word, 'palms', is one of the frogs he likes and, held barely aloft in his sister's straining embrace, he turns his hands towards the heavens, smiling.

The day rolls on, and the male chaffinches are all singing their heads off from the most exposed perches they can grab. Further into the forest, a red deer carcass has grown warm enough over this last week to hatch a generous seethe of bluebottle maggots. Melodious warblers, meadow pipits and common reed buntings hop about the wriggling buffet, the electricity of abundance eddying in their veins. A fox vixen curled in a nearby den licks her sore teats.

The children's father returns for the noonday meal, shedding his fellows towards the village proper. They will return later with a second horse, and all will re-enter the forest. The men will use the horses' muscles to drag the tree they felled that morning into the children's father's yard. They will use wooden mallets to drive wooden wedges into the lines of natural weakness at the end of the log. When the trunk opens up into planks, it will smell like toasted milk inside.

Family

NOT VERY MANY years ago, Hille – she is the mother – had sung lilting agrarian songs as she pushed barley into warm heaps on the floor of the malting house. She planted onion seeds and worried in a sweet, comfortable way about this, that and the other.

Craft – he is the father – had been congenial and happy-go-lucky. He was a man whose arms and eyes reached up more often than most people's arms and eyes: up to assess the height of a tree, up to saw the growth off the pollards, up to anticipate where a branch might try and clutch at its fellows to break its fall. His three sisters were all gone to their marriages, and the house by the forest made a kindly oblong around himself, Hille, their two children, and his old mother Sighrith.

When still a young woman, Sighrith had travelled from Denmark as the adored nursemaid of a ten-year-old girl, the girl being promised in marriage to the lord of the manor that SMV was beholden to. The lord had liked both the girl and the convoy of dowry goodies she'd arrived with, but he'd soon encouraged his bride to discard Sighrith in favour of a lady's maid of his own choosing. A respectable woodsman was arranged as a husband for the teen nursemaid, and to please the young noblewoman's soft heart, arrangements were also made for the couple to receive this good house by the forest.

Sighrith had liked her new husband. She had liked how his shoulders and back seemed to contain a whole oxen team – as will happen in some woodsmen with the right genes. After giving birth to Craft, she'd felt perturbed to see him grow only upwards. That is, until his sixteenth year, when he'd suddenly fanned out sideways like lichen on a log that has been rotated. Then he grew and grew, and soon his father shrank and shrank, and Sighrith did too, until the pair of them could have curled up and crawled inside their son's chest for a nap.

One day, Craft was laying flat stones into the floor of the saw-pit while Hille cut fodder for the cow. Sighrith sat in the house feeding her husband white cheese on rye bread sopped with broth. She lay down beside him and spoke to him in Danish. She rubbed his wheezing chest and then masturbated him while her mouth cupped his earlobe. He died that night, and Sighrith decided that she would like to die too, but that she would wait to help deliver Hille's second baby. After the boy was born, she waited some more because she saw how tired Hille became.

Hille waited too, desperate to go back to being the person she'd assumed she always would be. For three years, this is what she thought whenever she remembered that person: *I covet your easy buoyancy. If only I'd been warned, I would've made better use of it. I would've safeguarded you. I would've done more things that God would want me to do.*

When he turned three, Hans – he is the boy – started to follow Gretha – she is the girl – about on her chores, and Hille began to improve. She was like a tight bud sensing the day length changing and beginning to relax its cuticle in preparation for opening. Sighrith felt the shift in her daughter-in-law and finally allowed herself to die – and then the rain began to fall. Beneath the earth, her body went soggy, and the beetles and larvae who would normally have begun to eat it crawled to the surface to avoid drowning in the waterlogged soil.

Rain

Once upon a time, it should not have rained such a cold and ceaseless rain in SMV. It was, after all, June.

'This isn't what we expected,' said the snails, and dissolved the gates of hardened mucus they'd used to seal their shells against the expected heat. The rye was already bobbing with fat green ears, and the rain made the kernels swell and mildew. It also made the storks forsake the violence of the engorged waterways for the newly flooded fields where rodents and snakes floated on the water's surface, ready for the plucking. Some stork chicks died of cold in their nests that summer, but those that lived dined on a banquet of flushed-out dainties that saw them fatten like barons.

The wheat crop rotted even as it struggled to ripen. People squelched barefoot and barelegged along their furlongs and rescued what grain they could. Some made stilts and learned to use them, and others made up sarcastic, hopeful songs about turning into porpoises. Everyone wore mittens, right through summer.

In the beech forests, dormice gazed into their crystal balls and saw that the trees would not make good nuts the following year. They judged that they should skip having babies next spring and prepared to put themselves to bed for eleven months.

By the time the millpond froze over towards the end of autumn, the poorest cotters – who had little set by for a rainy day as long as this one – had begun to sell their few tools, then to beg and steal, then to fall down in the doorways of churches and monasteries, their empty tummies distended from lack of protein. Wasps froze in their nests and wolves' dens collapsed under the weight of the snow. When winter finally thawed into a sleet-filled spring, meadows normally bombastic with fifty kinds of flower showed only the shiny yellow faces of marsh marigold.

The second rainy summer arrived. It hardly mattered now what you had to sell; the cost of buying grain to make up your own shortfall made a joke of your profits. Clay daub grew so engorged with water that it slid off the walls of houses, leaving the lattice of hazelwood that had supported it as bonily exposed as the people within. Cattle and sheep's feet rotted in their pastures, or they contracted a cruel murrain that saw them begin to ooze about the eyes, mouth and nose. Men and women who'd known the creatures since they were all young together tried not to vomit from the stench that came off them. The animals eventually shat themselves to death, compulsively clamping their flanks even when their bowels were wrung hollow.

From Sweden came stories of splashes of light in the night sky that resembled showers of blood. In England, it was a glowing red crucifix that had hung in the heavens. Rain became a word more evil than Devil, and in SMV, the priest in the pine-floored church began cutting slices off the bottoms of the tallow candles and eating them before mass. They were the cheapest grade of candle, and had flecks of bone and flesh in them that he would get tastes of from between his teeth while he preached.

For a while, Craft and Hille fared better than most. SMV was pocked with tired wooden structures whose timbers came down in splinters as their foundations were carried away by successive downpours. Households whose animals had died of contagion burned the wooden buckets and mangers the creatures had eaten and drunk from and the byres in which they'd slept. Wood to rebuild with was needed faster than Craft could cut it, and even after paying what was due to the manor he found himself a man on the up.

Mindful of the thrashing his sawblade was taking from all the extra work, the woodsman bought a new one. He bought more pigs because everyone knew that pigs were little bothered by an excess of rain. And because horses weren't sickening in the same unbearable way as horned animals were, he bought a pregnant mare. Merely days later, clever Gretha noticed the first rind of discharge around their cow's eyes, and she ran back from the meadow to fetch Hille with a knife to cut the beast's throat before it tried to head home for the evening. Hille had already begun daily caressing the new mare's udder to get her accustomed to the milking to come. 'Gurgle, gurgle,' went the woman's empty innards as she mumbled prayers of gratitude into the horse's warm ribcage.

In the third awful autumn, when the time for harvesting hay came, its stalks were so wet that scythes bruised rather than cut them. The sun didn't peer through the clouds for long enough to cure what *was* able to be cut, and Craft and Hille brought their hay to barn still damp.

The nitrogen and moisture remaining in the hay became bread and ale for a festival of microbial life, whose metabolic activity produced so much heat that it ignited the methane they were excreting. The hay smouldered, the hay caught, the hay blazed. The rain eventually put the fire out, but not before the whole barn end of the cottage – and the year's pathetic harvest with it – had burnt to a husk.

Hille's heart fell back into the hole it had barely climbed out of.

The family sold most of their chickens and bought what grain they could get. Salt had quintupled in price as, without sunshine, the brine lay slushy in the drying pans for months on end. It cost so much to salt a side of pork that Craft slaughtered only one pig that year, then Hille used so little to season the blood sausages that they began to moulder within weeks of being made.

Because they didn't have enough oats to keep two grown horses through the winter, Craft sold his old stallion and began training the mare to pull logs. He watched as her breadth parted the veils of rain with a placidity he could no longer find in himself. The foal scampered along beside her and whickered nervously every time the harness clanged, but he was suckling less and less each day now, and the sweet, thin milk the family drank bowlfuls of each evening would soon dry up.

Craft and Hille didn't know it, but as the blackened timbers of their barn steamed in the drizzle, the Arctic ice castles stopped sending out quite so many carts of cold. Those already disgorged, however, continued their journeys into the North Atlantic, the North Sea, and even the Baltic, trading their chilly cargo for a final haul of terrestrial heat as they passed each landmass.

By the end of winter, one in seven of the residents of SMV was dead, and the rest were walking broomsticks. It was the same everywhere in Europe north of the Alps.

Storks

On the plains of East Africa the sun is orange and the moon is orange, and dry-season fires are driving storms of insects out of the grass. Storks follow them in orgiastic black-and-white feeding flocks the size of cloud shadows, gobbling up the fleeing chitinous bodies. At rest, the birds settle onto stomachs swollen with over a thousand locusts each and preen their smoke-reeking plumage. They think about how cold their northern breeding grounds have become, and whether or not to travel back so far this season.

The arses of Craft's children are very narrow on the bench by the table. *You are made out of vapour, only briefly now condensed into bodies*, he thinks. He sees the knobs of Hille's spine poking at her neck skin and has an urge to rub them with something fatty. *Everyone looks like this now*, he recognises, and it seems that the floor of the cottage has turned into a sea of mice that is heaving and bucking beneath his feet.

On their straw that night, the couple talk about the cooper's widow, who has drowned her one-year-old in the river in the hope of having enough to feed herself and her seven-year-old.

'Not all condemn her for the act,' observes Hille thoughtfully. The linen of her shift has lost its coarseness to age, and she is fingering its soft folds back and forth across her abdomen, testing the puckered skin beneath. Craft brings up the man who, terrified by having eaten the acorns he'd put aside for his pigs' winter confinement, was caught throwing into their sty the body of an itinerant labourer who'd died while mending thatch with him.

'Some say the angels will put their hands over God's eyes,' says Craft wonderingly, 'because the man has been pious and has gone regularly to mass all his days.'

In a neighbouring village, two charcoal burners have said that their brother fell down from hunger in a drift of the winter's final heavy snow, and that they couldn't pull him out with their own scrappy bodies. But Hille has heard that their eyes leapt hither and thither as they told the story, and grease was on their lips even though they were known to be amongst those living off pine bark and darnel seeds. 'The men probably snared some creature venturing too early out of its winter shelter,' says Craft, but he sounds unsure.

Hille's body keeps making small spastic movements next to him. She sits up, pushing her shift aside to show him the tiny fillets of muscle hanging from the underside of each thigh.

'Every time I look at these, I wish I could cut them off and cook them for the children,' she says. 'I haven't been able to sleep since Gretha began throwing up. She should be more still, I think. Flitting about like a lark is drawing the strength from her stomach – we must save her the first eggs when the chickens come back on the lay. The little red one won't lay again, I'm sure of it. See what you can get for her from the reeve.' Hille's mouth relaxes momentarily as she imagines the contents of the reeve's barn, and Craft wishes he could convince her to stop emptying her own bowl into those of the children.

He thinks, *Your eyes are bulging like a frog's, my love. You haven't even enough flesh to keep your eyes in.* His head feels as heavy as a sleeping horse, and he drags his wife to him and cries hard into her back, thinking about who in SMV might help him cart the freshly sawn planks to the manor house tomorrow. Curled like a dried pea pod, Hille dreams of young men with faces half-silvered like fishes', bearing her children away through the forest on large silver platters. The platters are heaped with food more luxurious than even the stuff on the high table at the manor's Christmas feasts. The children plunge their hands into baked custards, lift huge wedges out of richly spiced pies, and pull cloud-like fistfuls of soft white bread into their mouths, pausing only to dunk them in the running juices of roast partridge and swan.

Spring dresses the next day in flowers, and in the afternoon, when Hille's eyes have been empty of her children for a quarter arc of the sun, she scoops a bowlful of thin porridge from the pot. She aches to eat it like a tipped barrel aches to roll down a hill, but as soon as she thinks of their small bodies, she can't do it. She remembers how when Hans was a flapping, screaming baby, his puny body would relax only if he was pulling milk out of her harder than a calf. New grass is busting through the earth all around the saw yard, and Hille rips it up in handfuls and chews them fast and then slowly, laughing uncontrollably as she imagines a hare getting mad at her for eating its dinner. When the children get back with their baskets of kindling, she's sitting on a stool by the tiny window, staring at a half-mended fish trap on the ground between her knees. She is praying fast and loud.

Hans hates the noise of it in the dark smoky room and begins walking in tight circles around the hearth. Faster and faster he goes, feeling that his feet are glued to a beautiful, satisfying track that lets his torso lean inwards at a thrilling angle. His basket swings out and knocks the pot off the coals. Hille screams as though she's been kicked and lunges to scrape up the liquid from the ground. Gretha moves to help, but her mother slaps her hands away.

Pine martens are emerging from tree hollows to hunt little birds in the fading light. They gallop silently along branches, their Kewpie doll faces still bibbed by luxuriant winter neck fur. Craft approaches the cottage feeling as dizzy as a spindle and wondering how he will work another day without a bigger meal under his belt. Inside, Hans is lying on the floor mewling like a cat into hands cupped over his face, which is shiny with mucus and tears. Craft can hear Hille sloshing water into buckets under the middle part of the building's thatch – the part with the storks' nest on it. Gretha tries to tell her father about the pot and how Hans should get the stick, but the woodsman is thinking about all the animals they've traded away for grain, and how the absence of so many warm bodies sharing the house has left its bones cold and stiff. He crawls into bed without even shaking out the straw. As soon as he shuts his eyes, primary-coloured lights begin tumbling behind his lids, and Craft's mind returns to the origami he must construct out of the soggy paper of his family's situation. Yet again, the shape refuses to come out as it should.

A gut spasm hauls him from slumber. When he rolls over in the hope of unkinking the angry knot, Hille's open eyes are facing him in the dark, brighter than he's seen them in months.

She is – for now – less a sentient creature and more a matrix of cells engineering their survival out of what scraps they have to hand. Fault lines have opened up inside her and magma is spewing forth. Its white heat is engulfing her organs and blazing through the cracks in her face.

'I've been having an elaborate conversation with Christ all afternoon,' she says, 'and he tells me that we must put the children out of the way of this fate that now strides towards them as surely as a wolf claiming its kill. Craft, our Lord promises to take them into his arms if we send them to him. He will leave us just enough food that we might live. And when the grain ark is full again, he will give us another child to care for with our wholesome bodies. He says he will renew my strength as a reward for giving up what is most precious to me, and I will be able to tend to you and the new child as I used to before Hans was born. And you will be like a shining red deer, and will rebuild the barn better than before. God explained to me through his son that if we don't make this sacrifice, we will all starve before whatever harvest this next summer might grant.'

Craft gazes at her, his jaw slack with fatigue. He flexes his feet in anguish, his long, malnourished leg muscles impotently seeking some certainty of rebuttal. The roof of his mouth feels waxy, and he twists his tongue about on it like a snail looking for a way out of a jar.

Outside the cottage, a woodchuck murmurs on its branch and recurls a toe that has slipped on a loose piece of bark. Inside the cottage, the fire has died and the darkness is prickly with microscopic icicles, but Hille's head is burning as she moves closer to Craft and kisses him all over his cheekbones. He thinks that she can only have been given such radiance by something with more authority than the two of them. He imagines her happy again, and feels himself leaving that exhausting place behind his eyelids. He feels as he used to when he was warm and working well amidst the trees, looking up. He murmurs his assent.

Poor Gretha, you are not asleep, and your ears are like two abalone whose shells have just been flooded by a parasite-laden current.

Pee

In seven hundred years' time, there will be people who have never pissed outdoors. Unlike Gretha, they will not know the many-stranded golden magic of the pause enforced by the act: ten breaths spent watching your water dismantle frost crystals, push ants from their intended paths, or inundate a beetle – which then emerges miraculously dry on the far side of the flow. Tonight, the girl watches the hot liquid disappear into the skin of the earth while her parents' whispered words bang cymbals together inside her head. Tomorrow she and Hans will be taken far into the forest by their father and left there. They will be eaten up by bears, wolves or wild pigs and, according to Hille, will feel no pain because their innocence and God will make it so. Craft had asked Hille if she would eat a serve of pottage with him when the deed was done, and Hille had smiled audibly and said, 'It will be easy then.'

Only Craft could see how the woman's eyes were slipping from side to side in her glowing face like a clock pendulum.

The piss drips have dried between Gretha's legs, but she hangs in her squat a moment longer, looking at how brightly the moon glares off the white stones near her toes. They are chips of quartz, ferried by her own small, chapped hands from a special bend in the riverbank to make patterns with against the dark ground of the yard. Only yesterday Hans had wanted her to make a giant star pattern. 'To help the storks find the house again,' he'd explained.

Gretha had scoffed at the idea. 'They don't need a star, silly. They can smell their own nest even from up in the sky. Like a dog can smell out a dropped fritter in the marketplace. What do you think they have such long noses for?!'

There are still no owners of long noses in the nest on the roof, however, and the girl is unobserved as she gathers the white stones into a pile by the empty pigsty.

Quartz

'COCK-A-DOODLE-DOO!' SAYS THE rooster, but the woodsman's household is already wide awake. Hille is walking back and forth by the open shutter, having taken up her praying where she left off. Her eyes are still going tick-tock, but her cheekbones drenched in the dawn's pink light strike Craft as an affirming portent, and he pushes past his writhing intestines and through the tar of his brain to instruct his daughter. He tells her to wrap a portion of bread for herself and Hans because they're to come to the forest with him today.

'There's a fallen elm I have a mind to bring in for firewood. It's good and cured, and not too wet neither after these two dry weeks. I'll have its branches all off in one day, and then it will pull prettily enough. And there's ground elder and sweet cicely in plenty close by, so bring a cloth to keep them apart from what kindling you'll get into your baskets. And take your cloaks, for the spot is far enough that the air will be nipping by our return.'

Craft is desperate for his children to be as comfortable as possible until they are taken into the next kingdom.

Here they are on the shortcut path to the river crossing, pushing single file through the encroaching bracken. A creamy breeze sweeps in from the direction of SMV, carrying the tongue-click of wood being chopped. Hans must walk at the rear, for he always must, and will weave around legs and headbutt kneecaps if he's placed anywhere else. For this reason, and because he'll be expected to dawdle, Gretha has given him the white quartz stones. And she has taught him a game. Words can't convey how excited Hans is about this game, and it's hard to prevent him setting to it before they've even left the yard. 'You can start when we get across the river, Hans,' hisses Gretha, and retrieves another stone he's just dropped onto the path. But only a dozen paces later she hears him whisper noisily to himself, 'Chop up the lard to make a big pie, hey!' and drop a stone on the 'hey' – just as she has practised with him.

As they approach the roar of the water, Craft halts amidst the bracken, his broad chest floating above the sea of stiff auburn fronds. 'Why do you hang back so?' he calls, and he sounds worried and like a victim. His daughter calls back that Hans has seen the sunlight flashing off the silvered thatch of the cottage and thinks it's a stork who has landed there and is waving goodbye with its wing. 'He won't stop turning around to wave back at it,' she complains – and all at once her father's stubbled face looks very stupid to her because she is discovering how to regard him as a foe.

By the time they enter the forest, Hans is playing his game with steady, hypnotic reliability, and Gretha stops retrieving the stones. Under the climbing sun the bits of quartz gleam as boldly as gobs of fresh cheese, but the girl worries that the dusk's lower light might not find them through the ceiling of nascent foliage, and her chest tightens every time the canopy does. The boy's 'heys' grow steadily louder, but Craft plunges onwards, hearing nothing over the creaking of trees and the waterfall of blood inside his head.

Storks

FINALLY, THE STORKS are on their way. They have converged above Egypt, cut across the southern end of the Gulf of Suez, skirted the eastern end of the Mediterranean. Wherever possible, they avoid the profligacy of flapping and ride the thermals instead. Those cushions of warm air only inflate above sun-warmed earth – not above water or night-time places – so the storks travel by day, adding extravagant distance to their route by swinging from landmass to landmass.

Most of the birds can't resist the tug towards the familiar and the established, and are returning to their known feeding grounds and precious nests. Others, many of whom have lost chicks to the abnormal weather of the last few summers, will seek to stop and rebuild at lower latitudes. Some alight on a nine-hundred-year-old aqueduct on the Aegean coast of Turkey and decide to stay. They begin to vie for the positions with the best views of the surrounding airspace – arching their necks back into U-bends as sharp as croquet hoops and thwacking the two halves of their bills together to produce a clattering sound. They have no pharynx in their throats, which renders them semi-mute, but they shriek quietly and stab furiously to defend their chosen nesting spots, sometimes goring their rivals so deeply as to cause a death-bleed. The most overbearing among them will be able to reclaim their new nests every spring for the rest of their lives, extending the structures annually until the largest of them weigh half a tonne. Nests will still be tended here seven hundred years in the future – sixteen hundred years after the Romans laid the aqueduct's last chunk of marble. People will flick through travel brochures and pause on the page showing photos of the site, marvelling at how extravagantly the storks have festooned the fragmented arches.

Most of the flock continues north. Imagine them now, a scattered formation of half a million birds, flying at the same speed that a horse gallops, the whole flock taking more than a month to pass any given spot. In the brusque updraft above Turkey's Kizilirmak Delta, they relax their pectoralis muscles and drop height to scan for the resting place. They descend onto the delta's wetlands like falling flakes of pale ash and scarf down minnows, shrimp and slim water snakes. They regurgitate the indigestible bits of shell, tooth and bone in pellets the size of Brida's big toe. They stand on one leg, tuck their long red beaks into their chest feathers, and sleep.

As they fan out across Europe, they clear mountain ranges at heights great enough to turn them into specks in the eyes of ibex. They are getting thinner, and impatient for the luxury of having all day long to forage and eat. They begin flying further and further each day until they're covering more than four hundred kilometres between sunrise and sunset. *I can't wait to see my mate*, thinks one female as she soars over a Transylvanian salt mine, and she refocuses her body into the best possible shape for speed. She has been flying for six weeks now, and every day the dull red of her bare-skin areas has grown a little more vermillion. Her mate's skin, half a country away, is performing the same trick. Each of them hopes to look beautiful to the other when they meet.

Terrain / Night

Gretha doesn't know this part of the forest. The ground is buckled, and the trees are mostly conifers so tall that she can hardly make out their tops. In every gully a young streamlet is eagerly helping the forest's older, more established watercourses distribute four years' worth of downpours. On the sharpest rises some trees have been toppled by storms, and light and air gush into the dimness from clearings skewered with trunks.

As the day strides onwards, there is honey on its breath. For Hans – who'd been a baby the last time there was a spring whose orchestra of blooms hadn't had its instruments ruined by rain – the smell is triumphant. He looks at the trees and thinks, *How very tall you are! Your phloem is mine too, drawn up through me by the eternal vacuum.* He looks at a magpie and thinks, *How black-and-whitely you dive! Falling like a church bell from out of the green needles, then down an angle that ends in water.* For a while now he has had no more quartz bits to drop, so Gretha has had her nose stuck in the book of the landscape, trying to commit its erratic verse to memory.

Finally, Craft stops. 'The place where you'll find those herbs lies not far beyond that stream down there,' he says. 'I go this way to the elm, but I'll come find you hereabouts when I'm finished.' He feels as though he must be visibly flickering as he says these last words.

Hans' brown curls are already jogging off in search of the sweet cicely, whose aniseed-flavoured fronds he adores.

The children wander among adolescent silver birch that have repopulated a hank of land-slipped hillside. They harvest what edibles they can find, although they see neither of those that their father had mentioned. As the sun straddles the high beam of the sky like a gymnast in golden lycra, Hans' eyes take on a doughy look that Gretha recognises. She wraps him in both their cloaks and lays down beside him while he sleeps.

The cold leaves below them whir and tick with beetles, spring-tails and earthworms busily tunnelling, chomping and mating. Hans breathes noisily through his mouth as he dreams, and the girl waits for Craft to change his mind and come get them. With goose flesh moulded from mortuary marble, she begins wondering what it's like to be eaten by a bear. She doesn't know about falling unconscious, so she visualises her legs being chewed up while her head and torso continue punching and screaming in protest. She imagines punching the bear's face until it spits her out, leaving her to a life with no legs. There's a one-legged man in SMV whom Gretha remembers Hille describing as fastidious to a fault. Craft doesn't like him either.

When Hans rouses, the children return to the stream to pick watercress. They hold their slabs of hard brown bread in the shallows until it's soft enough to chew, then crouch forward and scoop up water in their cupped hands to drink. Hans chokes until his face is red – as he always does when he drinks 'in the cat way' as Gretha calls it – but he keeps right on drinking. A fire salamander watches them from the dark mud across the water's gurgle, and Gretha meets its eye.

The warmth of the last week is dispersing snowmelt from the high country so steadily that the rocks on which the children crossed the stream this morning are now submerged beneath a speeding, glassy skin. By the time they find a better crossing, the light is sliding down the lower half of the tree trunks, and Gretha clasps Hans' hand and sets off hurriedly in the direction that Craft had taken when he left them. There is an unsteady fluttering behind the girl's sternum. It builds rapidly into a wild whomping of wings, and she begins yelling for her father, again and again, louder and louder, but the forest only froths softly with twilight twittering. Up and down the dips and humps she drags Hans, trying to rewind the terrain they'd covered after running out of stones. Dip and hump, dip and hump, like a rolling sea, and her brother's hand is so small and slithery with sweat that maintaining her hold on it is taking up half the focus she needs for orienting herself.

Then comes a dip with a white dot glinting in its belly. This dot looks so perfectly round that the girl suspects it to be an unseasonal puffball nosing through the newly thawed earth, but she tugs them towards it all the same. And it is a piece of white quartz, and then there is another one, and then another one. Hans has spotted them too and wants to stop to put each and every one of them back into his basket. If she tries to keep him moving, he kicks and bites, and his violence eventually outstrips her determination to reach known ground before nightfall. They walk on and on and on, and when the forest finally slides out of the circumference of the sun's influence, they stop and wait for the moon. Gretha stacks branches around them for warmth – and to use as weapons in case something with teeth comes sniffing.

No sooner does the moon rise than it swaddles itself in clouds as thick as silver fox furs, leaving the forest dark. The children make short forays into the blackness, kicking at the leaf litter to test if some white gleam might reveal itself, but they see only an earthworm with a weak green glow, twisting in the humus.

Ghosts

Light returns to the lands around SMV, and the last of the unopened daffodils roll back their buds' papery covers to allow their flowers to inflate. The children rediscover their trail of stones and follow it home.

If this story was *only* a story, their father would rush out to meet them and sweep them into his relieved arms. But it is both a story and a thing that happened on one side of the earth after a series of volcanic eruptions happened on the other side. And while the ghosts of those distant peaks now roil with life clambering its way back to fecundity, here by the woodsman's cottage, the lukewarm morning hangs densely around ghosts who are only this moment forming.

There is the ghost that is Craft's face with the blood falling out of it as he spots his tired offspring pushing their way up through the bracken. There is the ghost of Gretha's certainty, which includes the house: a thing that bears the same shape as the house she has known, but whose lack of safety renders it a disconcerting facsimile. Then there is the ghost-demon that will visit Hille to-night after a day she'll spend staring at her children with eyes like fixed discs. She won't utter a word the whole day long.

For now, the mouth in the ghost of Craft's face says, 'I searched for you all about the stream, but you must've wandered further than you realised.' Then he scoops up his teetering son and car-ries him towards the cottage. Gretha trails after them, her small shoulders heaving with sobs that seem to ricochet off her father's back. When he turns towards her and she sees his terrified face, the sobs amplify into full-blown bawling. She follows him blindly indoors like this and crawls dumbly into bed beside her brother.

All that afternoon, the wind bustles around the building, preparing itself for a storm. When they wake in the evening, Gretha is flushed and sticky, Hans needy. The dollop of dinner that the family pulls their benches up to soothes nobody, and as the air outside begins shoving the bones of the house around more aggressively, Craft enlists Hille's silent help to push the big oak table against the cottage door to stop it flying open in the gale. Gretha has already watched her mother empty Hans' basket, removing the bundle of pot herbs then tossing the white stones out into the yard.

Below the soft quaking of the thatch, Hille's mind is all wind-mills. They spin at a great clip as she assesses the tiny remaining quantities of grain and peas and the likelihood of an egg a day. She dreams a strobe-lit dream that she and the children eat the mare, in secret, down by the river. They're spreading the bits of meat with rancid butter and really enjoying them, when she remembers that without a horse they'll have no income, and rushes back to the cottage to break the bad news to Craft. She can see him clearly through the doorway, but as she enters he becomes a combination of the reeve and also the stallion that was the mare's father.

The reeve-stallion piddles green sap onto the floor, and Hille's adrenal glands flood her blood with stress hormones. She opens her eyes and tells Craft that they need to try again.

Bread

I LOVE YOU, I love you, I love you, Craft thinks as he lifts Hans onto the black mare the next morning, and the thought is at once for Hans and for Hille. The man doesn't see the absurdity of having told his children that they're going back to the forest to haul the elm in (these woodsman's offshoots know that a log can't be horse-pulled over such ground as they covered yesterday!). His wits are quite addled by the pinching of his innards, plus he is distracted by thoughts of the wild-goose chase on which he plans to take his children – from which he will need the horse to help him find his way home.

For the mare's sake, they take the longer, wider path to the river crossing. On either side of the hardened track, the yowling wind is flattening the new grass like something strained through fingers. Gretha has developed a cold, and her face is florid with fever. As they cross the broad wooden bridge that her grandfather led the villagers in building, the girl notices that the sweep's brush has begun flowering, and knows that those who still own cows will be moving them out to pasture. She starts crying again, and the mare's skin gives a shiver between her thighs. Four sets of protruding ribs head into the trees.

At the millpond by SMV, five ducks take off like wooden fans being tossed into the flapping grey sky. A pair of crested grebes brave the water's choppy surface to perform their elaborate sequence of courtship movements. They dip and weave their mohawked heads in perfect imitation of each other, forming Rorschach prints with the symmetry of their necks and wings. They pedal their webbed feet like ecstatic tap dancers until they are running on water. Nearby, a sweet chestnut tree thrashes in the palpitating wind. It's one of a handful that deigned to germinate in the vicinity of SMV during the four centuries of relative balminess. This one is three hundred and seventy years old and almost entirely hollow inside a ring of living tissue that swells into deep cyclonic furrows on its outer face. For four seasons now, neither this tree nor its relatives have produced any of their long strands of semen-scented flowers. It just wasn't possible amidst such wet and cold. The trees have started a journey towards mushrooms and mud, and their kind will soon disappear from these latitudes entirely.

Two hundred and ninety kilometres from the millpond by SMV, a male and female stork are homing in on their nest. The birds are still separated by a wide river valley and the swathe of clouds above it, but the gap is shrinking as they soften their bodies into the expectation of arrival, and this year will see them alight within hours of each other. The male looks down and sees great scars of exposed earth where rain has dragged all the topsoil off the steeper slopes that were cleared for cropping during the warm centuries. He sees limestone plateaus prickling with the green static of young juniper plants. The growth has emerged as the wild goats – who previously razed every shoot – have been hunted with new thoroughness by starving humans.

Twelve thousand, one hundred kilometres from the millpond, a tall sandalwood tree is growing in the jungle that now laps about the feet of the ex-volcano. A macaque squats comfortably on a limb of the tree, repeatedly burying its whole face in the sunset colours of a papaya, casually observing the green ants who are investigating the juice that has dripped onto the tree's elephant-hide bark. Being careful to crush their pincers between its fingertips, the macaque pops some ants into its mouth and relishes their citric sparkle against the dull sweetness of the papaya.

Four kilometres from the millpond, a black mare and two children are moving through the beech forest as one mass. When a roe deer is disturbed by their passing, Hans watches its white rump flash as it springs into the undergrowth. Unlike his sister, there is nowhere in him that connects the deer's anus with his own anus – his awareness of his body doesn't function that way. He also doesn't take in how Craft's eyes duck carefully past his and Gretha's faces when the man halts the mare to check her bad hoof. Gretha does though, and she understands the worst to be true.

A fox uses its teeth to pluck hoverfly larvae from the surface of a stagnant pool. The surface tension of the water reknits as the fox licks its lips. The humans and the horse pass a misfit holly amongst the erect beech trunks, and the children recognise it as the one that they try to re-find by its scarlet berries each winter. They love how its branches have drooped down to touch the earth and rooted again, forming a doughnut of hidden space. Below the soil's surface, the holly's root tips are being consumed by *Thielaviopsis* fungus that penetrated them during the long spells of waterlogging.

Up goes Gretha's courage and down goes Gretha's courage – like the wings of a stork flapping towards the next warm updraft. At first, she aims to compose her mouth behind her flood of tears, thinking to plead with her father to take them home. But the longer she watches his large, tense shape moving in front of her, the more she just wants him to think that she is good. Her cheeks dry very pink and tight.

The landscape is becoming a stranger now, and the girl unwraps both her own and Hans' portions of bread and places them in the V-shape formed where her hiked-up kirtle spans the mare's back. Whenever they pass a large rock, she squeezes with her knees to ask her mount to go more slowly, then swoops down with rodeo-star finesse and places a small chunk of bread atop the rock's flattest surface. The bread is brown against grey stone, and she knows that she'll never spot it if the light is bad, but that maybe Hans will because he's good at spotting things. He is also good at being a scapegoat, and when Craft barks at the children for falling behind, Gretha tells him that Hans keeps stopping the mare so that he can peer up through the trees at the sky – in case the storks are finally coming, flying over the forest on their way to the cottage.

After a long, zigzagged journey, their father takes the horse and leaves them. The girl tries to follow him at a careful distance, but there is Hans behind her, stumbling along on his five-year-old's legs, stopping to watch a hedgehog who has emerged from its leaf-nest to worry at its fleas. The sound of twigs snapping beneath the mare's hooves begins to recede into the scraping, squeaking, cracking of the wind-harassed forest.

Panicked, Gretha hauls Hans onto her back and breaks into an awkward run. She soon gets Craft and the horse in view again, but so does Hans. 'Kartin! Kartin! Kartin!' he shouts – this being the mare's name, as well as one of the word-frogs he likes best.

Craft turns. He floats dizzily while the two smaller humans catch him up. His body holds his bones like rotten leather, and he rubs his hands incessantly over eyes that blare like a startled doe's.

This time, he sends his offspring away pleadingly. 'You know I can't cut wood with Hans about,' he murmurs. 'It's all spruce where I'm headed anyway, so you'd have no hope of picking anything for the dinner pot.' He tells them not to wander beyond the sound of his axe chopping, but when they follow this sound to its source in the late afternoon, they find a cleverly tied branch, swinging against a tree in the wind.

Gretha & Hans

'Hush, hush,' says the sky to the black wind that has bustled about all that day, and stillness descends for a lulling hour. The air becomes dark amber stuff, dense with latent electricity. When the storm starts, it is like gangly giants crashing through paper walls in the sky.

The children have been wandering for hours, and as the cloud cover plunges the forest into a premature dusk, Gretha gives up all hope of finding even one chunk of their bread trail. The bread contains as many weed seeds, moth wings and weevils as it does grains of rye – something to suit the palate of every creature in the forest from wren to stag – and all the crumbs have been eaten up.

The ground has barely exhaled the stored and thawed water of winter, and it sogs up rapidly as the torrents of rain release themselves between the boughs. Hans' forehead quickly becomes floral with plastered wet curls. He breathes loudly with the concentration of movement, and slips constantly on the slimy leaves, his weight swinging on Gretha's hand. The children search for anything familiar – perhaps a rock or a particular matrix of path forkings. Then they huddle in a hollow tree, their woollen hose so heavy with water that they drag down their legs like puckered porridge skin. They watch a wild sow trot through the downpour with her three stripelings cantering after her, and Hans presses his mouth into Gretha's cupped hand and blows hot air there.

They wander the drizzling forest the whole of the next day.

By the following dawn, the storm has wrung the sky clean. The flea-ridden hedgehog has uncurled from beneath the skirts of a blackberry bramble and trundled out in search of millipedes. It doesn't know that virtually all the forest around SMV will be cleared for farming over the coming six hundred years, or that this farmland will be sprayed regularly with pesticides. It can't anticipate how these pesticides will saturate the bodies of the local insects and worms, causing hedgehogs to die at rates fifty times those at which the famine is currently killing humans.

Both storks have finally reached their nest on the roof of the woodsman's cottage. They've greeted each other with joyful screech-clatters, mating within minutes of arrival. They don't know that a man and woman are lying below them on a mattress stuffed with galium and sweet woodruff, and that the woman is weeping freely onto the man's chest as he rubs his thick fingertips through her hair. They don't know that after the woman gets up, she'll go to the barn end of the cottage and find that one of her three brown chickens has laid the first egg of the year, or that she'll sit down on the chaff-strewn floor and eat the egg raw.

She'll feel the yolk glug over her tongue, and will experience a surge of energy that allows her to try and picture her children in heaven.

The forest has once again collected more water than it can hold and is sending it down, always down, into the streams and eventually the river. The forest doesn't know that some of this water has just now carried away a fallen trunk that has bridged a roaring set of falls for decades. It doesn't care that Hans and Gretha have crossed this trunk-bridge not long before it was swept away.

From between her granite-edged lids, Gretha has seen a wisp of smoke floating across the sparkle of the morning (Hans sees a transparent white stork). The girl's nose is too blocked by her cold to smell the smoke at first, but now she sucks hard on the air and, catching a direction, follows it. The sky is beginning to show a wide, fresh blue through the treetops.

We are combs in the long wool, thinks Hans as he hangs off her hand, his weary knees buckling with every fourth step. They follow the smoke up a tangly slope and emerge into a large clearing.

Part 4

Once Upon a Time

THE CLEARING IS partly wrapped by a stubby cliff that collapses at one end into tumbled blocks. A handful of mature birch dot the gentle bulge next to where the children have emerged, and the ground beneath their white trunks is radioactive with bluebells. Small copper butterflies float through the sunlight like dust motes in a cathedral, and squirrels in auburn halos scamper up trunks. In the lower half of the clearing are two ponds fed by a trickling rock. By the larger pond are some mallards, their shining bodies settled complacently into the fine, short grass. The smaller pond, hardly broader than a well, is encircled by a moveable barrier of compressed brambles. From this bramble-protected pond is a path worn into the grass, leading to an overhang in the cliff. And there lies Brida's cave.

Brida's cave is not like that other cave – the one yawned into the foothills of a volcano that no longer exists. The great chambers of *that* cave would have clanged about the young runaway's head like saucepan lids and might well have pushed her away (despite the wonder of the stalactites and stalagmites, despite the companionable funk of the horseshoe bats). If it had been *that* cave where she'd stopped to think, she might have moved on within a day or two to seek another city, another village, another town where she could turn her labour into food, a roof and people to become tied to.

But this cave is not that cave. Its floor is an even bed of pulverised limestone. Its standing room can be crossed in eight paces – beyond which the surfaces contract into a sphincter that demands a crawl, then flare into a cavity that demands a stoop. Alongside the cold smell of reclusive earth, the animal musk of a lair is present – enough so that on her third day there, Brida had picked over the bits of bone in the rubble and inspected them for freshness.

The cave's walls are grizzled grey in some places and smooth and pale in others, but Brida has not taken up charcoal from her fire and drawn on these surfaces. There are a variety of buttresses and alcoves, but Brida has not decorated them with grass plaits or carvings – unless you count the spoons and lidded bowls that she has worked to a smoothness beyond any necessity. She has wedged two long poles across the roof space, and they dangle with baskets on lengths of twine that dismay all but the most nimble mice. She has carpeted the floor with dozens of rush mats, which creep up the walls in places where the slope invites it. She has hauled in rocks and logs of varying sizes for furniture, and over the years they have found their natural places.

Above her fireplace, she has made a narrow channel for smoke to rise through by burning out a fat tree root that had penetrated the roof. Immediately outside the cave's mouth, she has made a porch of woven willow and layered brush. This porch shelters a second fireplace and more useful logs.

It is on one of these logs that Brida has just placed a wooden dish of roasted filberts. Now she sets down another of baked apples.

As she's grown taller with adulthood and thinner with two decades of enforced fasting, Brida has begun to feel like some sort of wading bird. If she'd known of them, she might have begun to feel like a giraffe instead, but she doesn't know – has never even dreamt – of such a being. Her clothes have become dark with the kind of dirt that will never be kneaded out in pond water, and are patched in so many places that they look like an unopened advent calendar. Her felt hat – the pigman's felt hat – is soiled and tattered beyond recognition above her hard-boned face, and her hands are increasingly cramped by early arthritis.

She is indeed tall and thin. Perhaps if she'd lived in a time and place where she could not only *know of* giraffes but could eat an ice cream while gazing at one in a zoo, her height with some flesh on it would have made her imposing. Perhaps she would have become an actress and been cast as a hawk-nosed warrior queen in a TV historical drama. But in this time and place, she is scraping a hole in the forest floor with her digging stick.

This is a day where the swing of every animal's head is raw and holy, she thinks as the sky streams around her like freshly washed hair. She watches a robin flutter a liquid arc up off a bracken stalk to snaffle one of the midges who are rising from the warming ground. She finishes her morning crap and covers it with soil, then tilts up a rock that has lately been gathering snails on its underside. She knocks them into her palm to carry back to the clearing for the ducks. In seven heartbeats' time, she will see two children eating her apples.

Pork

IMAGINE GRETHA ASLEEP in Brida's big bracken nest, heat radiating from her forehead. The virus that has caused her cold is gallivanting through her sinuses, and the space behind her face is full of noisy red tunnels. Imagine Hans' unconscious limbs flung out next to her, his thumbs stuck up from his lightly curled fists like those of a tired hitchhiker.

Brida, your heart is a parrot, bursting with colours.

The sick child dreams in Fibonacci spirals, while outside the cave various climbers contract tendrils into tight coils, hoisting themselves closer to the sun. Brida waits all day long for her guests to wake up, leaving only to check the traps closest to the cave (no birds, three mice) and to bring the mallards inside at dusk to keep them from foxes. She thinks about the time when, during one of her early autumns in the forest, she'd found a dead mother boar with babies nosing around her still-warm nipples. The sow's hind leg had been broken in a shredded, infected way, and maggots were already swimming around her Achilles tendon. Brida had stayed up all night, luring the piglets home with her by dragging their mother's body before them, then building a barricade to block off the cavity at the rear of the cave – the same space that she has just waved the ducks into. Not until she'd fed the orphaned piglets mashed turnip off her fingertips did she begin to butcher the sow. It was only the third big animal she'd ever cut up, and the herculean focus it had asked of her underslept brain had seen Brida – after the job was finally done – fall asleep beside the babies on the bedding she'd tossed into their alcove, their small grabbing mouths still licking their second feed of mash from her fingers.

Over the week that followed, she'd eaten pork until her intestines begged for a rest, and it had been wonderful. She'd slept with the piglets every night, relishing the shared island of warmth as intensely as they did. Several of the little creatures had struggled to digest food that wasn't sow's milk and had quickly died.

When Brida had realised that the pork hanging above her fire wasn't taking the smoke well enough to preserve it, she'd shut the piglets into the cave, donned her male clothing, and walked over hill and dale to reach an alehouse in a bustling crossroads village. She'd traded the pork for barley, salt and broad beans, slept the night in the barn end of the alehouse, and began walking home by moonlight the next morning. She'd arrived at last light to find the remaining piglets all dead for want of her body heat. Oh Brida, how you'd looked forward to seeing them! You felt as though your heart had been plunged into a winter river.

Now the mallards are settled snugly in the alcove, and Brida drags into place the door of thick brush panels that she has made for the cave mouth. She sits down beside the two children to stare at them some more while they sleep. The cave is dark aside from the lurching firelight, and the gloom hides the thin milk that floats behind Brida's pupils – cataracts that are forming as a result of exposure to quicklime dust. Hans' and Gretha's faces glow as softly as peaches, and the woman looks at them through vaselined lenses and thinks a hundred thoughts.

The fire pops as it discovers a pocket of resin in the branch it is consuming. A jumping spider makes its way along the tracery of dead bracken near Brida's ankle, its eyes bright as pin-sized flashlights in the reflected light. Hans rolls up to sitting and pushes the heels of his hands into his face. He looks about and begins to speak. 'Oh no,' he says. Then he says it again. 'Oh no, oh no, oh no, oh no.'

And from that moment on, there is no peace for Brida.

Teeth

ONCE UPON A time, the night can smell the sun coming. 'Not long now,' say the dimmer stars, and wink at each other in the blackness while they still can. In the forests below them, beneath the decomposing mulch, the porous molasses gives birth a million times a minute. Brida is dreaming that some tree roots have revealed themselves to be nothing more than honey covered in a skin of blackberry seeds. Gretha lies trapped beneath her fever, her torso sometimes reeling up from the horizontal – like the waking of a cinematic vampire – to rattle the stillness with her cough. Hans is in the mallards' alcove, trapped by a large stone that Brida has rolled into a position where it blocks most of the entrance. The ducks bother him if they brush against his skin unexpectedly, but apart from that he likes it in there.

When the sun rises, Brida will peer around the imprisoning stone and see the boy lying on his back with his pelvis hiked up into a bridge, kicking all the bedding-bracken into a pile against the wall. Two pale, crushed circles will be visible amongst the smashed fronds, and Brida will know them to be duck eggs. A red prickle will crawl out across her freckled chest, and she'll heave the stone aside to drag Hans out by one of his feet. He will respond by biting her arm.

He'd bitten her last night too, when she'd tried to stop him from playing with the hairs on her calves. His vocal fractiousness had finally abated, and Brida – whose hands know how to do many things in near darkness – had been sitting by the dying fire twirling spruce roots into cord on her thigh. Hans had been lying at an angle to her with one arm stretched towards her gabled knee, like a swimmer at the moment of maximum extension. He was using the flats of his fingers to rouse her leg hairs into standing, then waiting for them to relax before doing it again.

Brida's eyes are still good enough that they'd observed the moony grin the boy wore as he watched this animation. But they aren't good enough to have seen what Hans saw: how each platinum hair caught the firelight and glowed like an electric filament.

Teeth II

'WHERE DO YOU get your grain?' asks Gretha. She is sitting by the outdoor fire and watching Brida change the water in a pot of barley.

Just as Hille would do, and as Brida's own mother would have done, Brida collects the cloudy liquid that she drains off the soaked grains and makes a drink by mixing it with whatever sweet things the season has provided. During their soaking, the water has penetrated the barley seeds' hard outer coatings, convincing them to start growing. Enzymes have sprung into action in the seeds' endosperms and have begun converting starches into the kind of sugars that a sprouting seedling needs for energy. This change has also made the nutrients in the barley more accessible to a human body.

'You don't go to the village,' adds Gretha, meaning SMV, and Brida looks quickly at the girl before replying, 'I go to Gutendorf. Over the escarpment.' She gestures towards the long chalky face that is the crescendo of the forest's mangled climb away from the valley that holds SMV.

When Gretha protests at the length of the journey, Brida adds twigs to the fire beneath the birch sap she's boiling and says, 'I prefer it that way.' She skims scum from the liquid's surface with a broad alderwood spoon before elaborating, 'The brewster at the alehouse there always gives me fair exchange for what I bring her. And she tells me where there's a few days' labour to be done so that I might come home with more than just what her stores can spare.'

Brida thinks about the brewster's two front teeth, which always show large and white in the dimness of the tavern's back room. The face around the teeth is broad and bloodshot brown, the eyes above them deep-set and the colour of dark ale. The first time that Brida brought goods to the tavern, those eyes had flicked consideringly over the triangular planes of her face, and she'd bent towards her baskets so as to hide behind her dirty, sunburnt forehead. The brewster had accepted the juniper berries, rejected the oak galls, and said that the squirrel skins should have been scraped more thoroughly before being dried. A month later, Brida is back with chanterelles and horseradish, and her squirrel skins are as clean as whistles.

Since then, she'd gone to Gutendorf several times a year, sometimes even in winter if the freeze hardened the mud and snow enough for walking. She remembers climbing a knoll to check her direction on one of these winter journeys and then looking down to see wolves racing across the snow like black wave crests racing across a white ocean. She remembers finding a forearm-sized trout swimming in some water that had collected in a deeply rutted track – though there were no lakes or streams within shouting distance. She remembers the time she'd sat down to eat with the brewster's household, including her husband the furrier and five of the pair's nine children. An old rottweiler had lain at the table's end and made rumbling noises in its thick throat every time the husband had thrown an arm around his wife's shoulders.

She remembers once – only once – having shown up at the tavern with a lynx hide. How the brewster had squelched her tongue against the back of her big teeth as she'd flipped the skin over to survey the tawny coat for blemishes and found none. Time stops there in that room while the grain is parcelled out.

Now Gretha is coughing again, her chest rattling like a barrel of acorns. Hans is leaning hard into the expanse of rock beside the cave mouth, slowly rolling his body over its undulations. Each time the cool, gritty surface meets his brow, he makes a long stop to enjoy all the information it contains. Gretha detaches her brother and enlists his help to gather firewood, and Brida watches the way the boy halts and stabs at the earth repeatedly with certain kinds of sticks. He stops only when Gretha – coughing all the while – reminds him of their task. Later, he pulls down a basket hanging from one of the cave's rafters, scattering beech nuts everywhere. Brida shuts him in the ducks' alcove again, and Gretha is not overly perturbed, because Hille and Craft often use the family's benches to shut him under the big table when there are no spare hands to keep him in check.

The girl nods off while her white blood cells continue mopping up the mess left by her cold, and Brida sets off to check how far the water level in the surrounding gullies has dropped since the rain stopped. She badly needs to set these children on their way. She can no more afford to feed them than their parents can.

Denmark

'HOW COME YOU have a Danish name?' asks Brida of Gretha when they're sitting below the porch again. Brida is sifting the detritus out of some fine ash that she'll use for making lye, keeping a hawk eye on Gretha while she does so. She has set the girl to chopping the rotten bits from the last of autumn's wrinkly apples and doesn't trust that she won't cut too much away.

A rude, musky waft threads its way between them as a shrew uses its anal glands to mark a trail through the nearby vegetation. The creature's heart is beating nine hundred times a minute – faster than a hummingbird's – and its metabolism is so hectic that it could starve to death after only a few hours without food. Instead of hibernating over winter to conserve energy, it has reduced its need for food by shrinking its liver, brain and even its skeleton by two thirds of their summer volumes. They are now regrowing daily.

'My grandma came from Denmark, and she was the one who named me,' replies Gretha, and Brida begins asking questions about this. She asks how long the sea voyage took, if there were whales, and whether the boat went as fast as a horse walking, trotting or galloping. Her image of the coast comes from its description by the seafaring husband at Rotting Splintering; she pictures sand being swallowed by water again and again with no clear place for either, and asks how people got from the boat onto the land. She asks how many horses carried the party southwards and if they met trouble, and about the cloth of each persons' dress – then she imagines her father handling the fabric and mocking the weaver's mistakes.

Each answer sends a fresh question bobbing to the surface, just as has happened when she's found herself working beside men who've seen far-off places and has dared to join the curious banter with her too-light voice.

But Brida – how different this is from being out in the world dressed as the pigman! Your words can scuttle out of you without risk here, and after each new crumb of information, you frown with the pleasure of working out where to keep it and what it's missing.

At first, Gretha likes saying everything she knows, but then she grows bored because she doesn't have the answers to lots of the questions. She wishes the rain – which has returned in the night with a vengeance – would ease so that she could leave the porch without soaking her kirtle. Brida has said that once this new downpour exhausts itself it will take some days for the gullies to become passable again, but that she'll then show the children their way home.

The ducks are floating on their pond amidst the surface fizz of pummelling raindrops. Hans is still shut in their alcove. He likes how there is nothing in there that isn't visible to him. 'It takes five trees to build a house,' he tells the wall of the alcove, and then he imagines saying it to Brida, this thing he has heard his father say.

Stew

The rain continues all through the next day, and when Brida wants to check her traps or collect fiddleheads and ground elder, she pulls off her clothes and leaves them beneath the porch before entering the wall of water. There she goes, feeling her way through the blur, Gretha looking at her wide-shouldered, sinewy body. She's intrigued to see that this person with the shortened, unveiled hair does indeed have all the parts of a woman.

In the afternoon, Brida kills the last of the pigeons that she has been keeping in a big wicker cage, and the girl sees how the woman's swollen knuckles cramp around the bird's plumage as she plucks it. Gretha holds her hand out for the lolling corpse and finishes the job, talking proudly about the sackful of feathers that her mother is saving for when people have money again to buy such luxuries. Hans is moaning tunelessly out under the porch, shifting from one foot to the other, obstructing Brida's way every time she needs to go outside and causing her to trip and gash her shin as she sidesteps him. When the stew is cooked, Brida is careful not to include any good bits of meat in the boy's serving.

'Crackle, crackle,' goes the hearth fire. Gretha breaks the ends off a pigeon bone and uses it as a straw to suck up the broth, then she gives it to Hans in case he wants a go.

Brida slurps her bowl clean as she thinks of the animals she could keep if she had Gretha here to tend to them while she went to work the harvests. Her pancreas releases a plume of digestive juices at the idea of all that protein, and her mind flies to thoughts of the cheese she'll eat when she next goes to Gutendorf. Two weeks more of sun, and bird scarers will likely be needed for the pea crop, not to mention weeders for the spelt. And if she can't get work in the fields, she can travel further and go to the limeburners again – though she always rubs her eyes reflexively when she thinks of the spitting vats of newly-slaked lime.

She anticipates sawing her dark blonde hair back into a masculine bob before placing the ends in her pillow sack with all the previous choppings (and reflects for a moment on what a poor sheep she'd make). She imagines putting on the short tunic and breeches and feels the sharp thrill of difference buzz through her, just as it used to in SMV when she'd change into her good kirtle for church.

The rain is not cold, but it will fall for two more days. In the streams and ponds, female newts are individually wrapping their eggs in the leaves of water weeds, and spadefoot toads are sitting on rocks, shining like lacquered seashells as they watch the water rush around them. Brida dreams that she and the brewster sit opposite each other on two wooden boxes full of important metal objects. The woman's mouth opens a smile like it knows all of Brida's insides.

Gretha dreams about Brida. She wears bark shoes on the wrong feet, and is as tall as a bell tower.

Strawberries

ALL THREE HEAD down the slope beyond the birch grove towards the banks of wild strawberries that grow there, and it could almost be a picnic. The light air that fondles their necks seems to diminish gravity, and Hans' young hand in Gretha's feels as soft as rose flesh. Above the depeopled clearing, a buzzard circles, setting the mallards to quacking offendedly as they waddle into the cave. A stoat is climbing a twisted hawthorn tree to get at a blackbird nest. It is already wearing its new warm-season chestnut coat, but the harsh winter has seen its body reabsorb the embryos of all but one of the kits it would soon have given birth to.

The tiny strawberries are as sweet as syrup! As the air has dried, the fruit have expunged the water that had threatened to burst them, and their tightened cell walls throb with phytochemicals so fragrant that they're making Hans woozy with pleasure.

'They're not for now; they're for later,' Gretha tells him as she models collecting cupped handfuls and tipping them into the bowl, and he does just as she demonstrates. When they find fruit that have been mashed by the downpour, Brida and Gretha eat them so as not to contaminate the rest, and the fermented red flesh smears warmly in their mouths. 'They're not for now!' protests Hans each time, and makes his annoyed shape of his palm at them.

Brida looks at him suspiciously, surprised by this new manifestation of a creature she has already decided is insensible to reason.

Far above the forest where violet echoes through the cobalt, the wispy cirrus clouds are growing even wispier. The three people work the strawberry patches right down the slope because no one wants to lose the rain-damaged fruit to rot. Brida observes how quickly the children's nimble fingers are filling the bowl. She stops them to divide some of the harvest up for eating, taking the larger share for herself. Hans loads his share into his mouth as though stoking a kiln, and then sits absently on Gretha's lap and gazes upwards. A trillion fragments of green stained glass glow against an eggshell-blue sky.

Gretha finishes eating, hoists the boy onto her back and stoops to continue picking as a four-armed animal. Her brother's legs hang slackly over her bum as she rolls her ribcage one way and then the other to dangle his hands towards the strawberries. He giggles ecstatically, then complains urgently, and she lets him down. Beside him is a young beech tree – barely older than Brida. Its trunk is lightly fluted, and its glowing canopy is humming with spring catkins. Once, in imitation of what she has seen men and women do together, Brida had kissed this tree, holding its smooth wooden cheeks in her hands. When she'd pulled away, a small patch of bark was dark and sticky with her saliva, and ants had already smelled the moisture and were heading towards it. She'd watched until they were drinking, then left.

Back in the clearing, the stoat has seized its chance and crunched through three blackbird eggs before being driven off by the father bird. Down amongst the strawberries, Hans pees into the spongy earth, and the hot, salty liquid kills a wireworm beside his foot. A red stag steps back into dappled cover as the humans draw closer.

Gretha begins asking Brida questions. Brida answers them because she has little talent for evasion when she isn't wrapped inside the gruff monosyllables of her pigman, and Gretha picks and unpicks the woman's replies, tugging at loose ends until she can weave them into the emerging design. She exclaims at Brida's readiness to leave her home village – a place the woman describes as 'very far away' – and Brida fails to discover words that could explain her decision to the girl. Gretha invents narratives demonstrating how Brida might have redeemed herself in Rotting Splintering or maybe elsewhere in the city where that house stood – and Brida is taken aback by how few of them have ever occurred to her. The woman dislodges a chunk of resin from the base of a spruce tree. Dropping it into her basket, she knows that tomorrow she will melt this resin with shredded bark to make fire-starter patties. She'll also mix it with lard when she has any to spare again, and will rub the resulting ointment into her inflamed knuckles.

'I'm content enough here,' she states. And they both see that it's true.

Seven hundred years after the time in which this story is set, people will mentally chart their success in relation to an elusive state called 'happiness'. This is not yet common practice in the time in which Brida, Gretha, Hans, Hille and Craft live. Instead, 'piety' is the coveted mirage. But as God increasingly seems to Brida like a resident of peopled places, she thinks no more about her obligations to him than she does about her obligations to the men for whom she labours when she goes down into the surrounding villages. She has her measures though. Autonomy is first amongst them. Then food. And right now, her mouth is contentedly lush with fructose. She leaves Hans and Gretha and goes picking her way across the slope to peer down at the falls. She has already checked the flow in the gully nearest the clearing and decided that tomorrow she will take the children home. Gretha wants her to come to the cottage to meet Hille and Craft, but Brida is adamant that she'll only go with them so far as is needed.

She pauses to listen to the distant barking of a doe. Drifts of bears' leek cover the acid soils further down the hill, and their garlicky smell crashes over her as it is chairlifted up the incline by the warming air. She moves into the broad break in the forest's skin that announces the falls and feels fine droplets gusting upwards from the whitewater below, the shining sky like melted butter on her eyelids. *Here I go into the bloom,* she thinks in chorus with the spray. *Into the gloaming, oiled blue.*

As the narrower section of the falls comes into view, it is momentarily obscured by vapour and rainbows. Then the light changes, and Brida sees that the log crossing is gone. She makes her way back to Hans and Gretha with butterflies in her bone marrow from the stress of it – but also for the reprieve.

Gravity

That night they dine on slugs and snails. It's been four days since they shared the pigeon, and Brida's traps and nooses haven't caught anything in the meantime – her hands and eyes are becoming too blurry for the job of setting them.

Before and after their viscous dinner, Gretha says prayers – as she has done at every meal they've eaten with Brida. Mostly Hans copies her. When he doesn't, she pulls him onto her lap and rocks him violently against her body, saying the lines like a metronome until he repeats them to her satisfaction. Tonight, he sits intently arranging the discarded snail shells along his shins, and he takes up the words seamlessly, matching their rhythm by pumping his solar plexus back and forth like a saw blade. High on the wall beside him, the cocoon of a cave-cross spider is bustling with spiderlings preparing to leave their winter haven. When morning comes, the first tiny bodies will bumble their way out through the silk mesh and move towards the light of the cave mouth. Some will reel out gauzy filaments and balloon off in search of new caves, and some will turn back into the gloom and make their lives metres from where they were hatched. Every spring Brida watches them, wondering how they decide who'll do which.

The children waggle their toes by the fire's embers, and Brida explains how difficult the journey back towards SMV is by any route other than across the falls. 'Better that we make a new bridge,' she says, and Hans pictures how the tree they'll cut down will fall in relation to the various angles of wedge that the axe might bite from its trunk.

The three bodies pull towards the centre of the earth as they sleep. Gretha's eyelids quiver as she dreams that she's walking with Brida on a path through the furze when Hille appears, coming from the opposite direction. When they meet, Gretha begins to introduce the two women, then realises that neither can see the other.

Brida dreams about the brewster again, and this time a clear parody of their first meeting is in action. Brida presents her squirrel skins but is mortified to realise that they are simply birch bark cutouts with bits of her own chopped hair gummed onto them with tree resin.

'Close, but no cigar,' says the brewster – and it's strange that she should say this, given that the phrase won't emerge from the fairgrounds of North America until early in the twentieth century. But no stranger than her speaking English. Or than this story's use of such words as 'Sweden' and 'Turkey' to denote parcels of geography and power whose names and borders didn't yet exist in 1317.

This storyteller isn't concerned. Everything outside of solipsism is an act of translation, and there is more danger in the illusion of veracity than in the degree to which it is pursued.

Brida wakes and sits up in the dark – maybe because her hollow stomach is squelching with underemployed gastric juices; maybe because there are birds chattering their alarm calls near the cave. She wonders if a fox might be after something caught in her traps. With dens full of young to feed, the vixens are always bolder than usual at this time of year and will come in this close to raid. Sometimes snare after snare is left holding nothing but a torn-off rabbit foot, and Brida must scour the forest for saplings she can bend into spring-loaded mechanisms that leave the ensnared animals dangling high above the ground.

Now she pulls on her surcoat and steps into the night, the soft ripple of Gretha's snores receding behind her. There are indeed two yellow eyes bobbing off to the side of the clearing, reflecting all the world's light back at her. She hurls rocks in their direction until they swivel and are extinguished. When she checks the snares that the eyes were nearest to, they're unsprung and empty.

The moon is always brusque with the hungry, and it tailors its reprimand to the observer. Tonight, it answers Brida's upwards glance with nothing more than, 'I am the barefaced moon.'

The woman pads silently back to her bracken nest and folds herself up to wait for dawn.

Choppings

First chopping. They stand by the falls. Brida swings her axe at the tree one, two, three times, then pauses to catch her breath. Her limbs are as weak as wool and will stay that way until she eats a good meal. The woodsman's children stare with bemused eyes at the cut she is making, and after a moment Gretha steps in to draw with her finger how it should go. Pride doesn't occur to Brida; she adjusts her angle as instructed and swings again.

They've chosen this tree because it grows by the narrowest part of the falls and because it's an elm, which shouldn't rot in the spray. Brida switches sides to begin the cut that will turn the trunk into a hinge, and Gretha darts forward again to correct her. 'Creak, creak,' says the elm when this second cut is finished, and Brida looks up the tree's grey height, wary of continuing. But Gretha and Hans wave her on unconcernedly, both merry with their expertise now.

The woman works her axe until her corrugated breastbone is brilliant with sweat, and down comes the tree. They all scramble frantically through the undergrowth, then watch as the arc of the falling canopy makes the whole bleached sky seem to swing away from the horizon. Critters rain down or fly up from their places in the foliage. The elm's head crashes onto the far bank, bounces once and rolls down into the funnelling water, which swivels the whole trunk like a clock hand until it topples off the gorge's edge entirely.

That afternoon, Brida instructs Gretha on the setting of traps. Twice now she has sent the girl out with the slingshot, but has discovered that she scarcely knows how to use it. Brida adds this to the other simple skills that Gretha seems unpractised in, and is puzzled. The woman's unsocial brain doesn't work in such a way as to deduce that Gretha's main task has always been to mind Hans – and to keep him out of the way of the very people who might have taught her anything.

But the girl learns quickly and energetically. By the time their sprinkle of grain has swollen in the pot of simmered greens (there is everything in there from violet leaves to the pith of cattail shoots), Gretha has dotted the bracken around the clearing with coyly concealed nooses and daintily propped-up rocks.

✕　✕　✕

Second chopping. They stand by the falls, and they are as hungry as lions. Their hunger doesn't roar but wears them away with its long, rough tongue, leaving behind only a dulling want plus the waves of adrenaline needed to serve it. Despite the promising start to spring, most everyone in Northern Europe is still this hungry. So hungry in fact – or so dead – that only a handful of the rain-ruined houses and roads are being repaired, and forests are no longer being chopped down.

As the plague and wars of the rest of the fourteenth century kill even more of the human population, some villages will be abandoned entirely. Their surviving residents will glom themselves onto whatever family they can journey to, and the fields they leave behind will start to grow woody plants again. Bird poop full of bramble and gorse seeds will sprout, and these pioneers will create a sheltered layer of moisture and fertility in which poplar, rowan and birch trees can take root. Once such fast-growing species have rebuilt the soil into something rich and sturdy, the slower oaks, beech and elms will claim their places.

Brida swings her axe one, two, three times. Young spruce cones rain down about her, and the scent of bruised terpenes decorates the air like tinsel. Just as physics sings to this storyteller via the pot of beans cooking on her stovetop (she can hear them now, like a Lilliputian orchestra warming up), physics causes the spruce to come down at such an angle that it dangles barely halfway across the falls. The white current froths about the foliage on the underside of the tree, and the wettening weight of it rips the trunk from its stump with a splendid crack. The splintered end tilts momentarily skywards as the whole tree slides over a rushing lip of water and into the churning below. 'Splosh, splosh,' go the tree's shaggy branches as they do battle with boulders in their path.

'You should have listened to Hans!' shouts Gretha over the roaring falls. 'He's very clever about how a tree will go down.' But Brida only flicks her a look of incomprehension and lopes off up the slope, mute with exhaustion.

Gretha sees that – like most people – Brida doesn't register as speech the downcast mumbling that Hans kept up for the duration of her chopping. He's still at it now as he pushes through the undergrowth along the edge of the gorge. He stops at every tree that has made its home within spitting distance of the rim, checking its shape and height. He looks across the water and sees how things are there. He works out which tree will be best, tells himself about it, then continues his explanation for Gretha, who has made her way to his side. He wants to go get Brida so that she can use this perfect tree to make the bridge right away, but Gretha says that they have to let her rest and sharpen the axe.

It feels so urgent to Hans to see his tree perform the fall he's imagining for it that he overflows into a tantrum. His sister wrestles him into the open by his elbow and bares his thin butt over her knee so that she can thwack it with a stick. Then, she folds him tightly against her chest and coos into the top of his blubbing, hiccuping head as he repeats what he'd tried to tell Brida while she was cutting the spruce.

The siblings hold hands and make their way quietly back up the slope. When they get to the clearing, Brida is squatting by the duck pond, rocking on her heels as she stares at the emerald shimmer of the drakes' heads.

Brida, think of the day you found the eggs that became these shining creatures. Think of the pike like a huge broadsword in the river, grabbing the head of the mother mallard as she tilted below the water to dabble for snails on the streaming weed. Think of how you grimaced to see her resurface with her bill half torn off and one eye punctured. Think of how you watched her reach the shore and then pushed your way through a lattice of suckering willow to twist her neck. When you finally found the nest, one of the eggs was rocking – and then they all started doing it, like a craze breaking out. Chinks appeared in their perfect armour and egg teeth started to butt at their membranes from within, widening the holes with the intensity and certainty of a sunrise. These days there are four generations to your little flock, and when you drop bundles of nettles and comfrey about their pond, the sound of their curious voices exploring their fodder is as acute to you as human words. When you return home, they greet you more fondly than a cat, if not so fondly as a dog. The nutrients in their shit-soiled bedding feeds your small garden, and the self-replenishing supply of blue-green eggs is more precious than a single duck-dinner could ever be.

Now, the afternoon sun has burnt off the sky's low fug, and Brida falls asleep on the grass. Stonechats are whizzing about the bracken. They pepper their syrupy chirping with tiny clicks – two snooker balls colliding at speed. At the foot of the distant escarpment, pregnant bison cows drag their massive bellies through the grass. The children watch the clouds, doze, and watch the clouds some more. Gretha thinks, without realising it, about her parents. What their faces might be like when she and Hans arrive home. How *she* should be, depending on those faces.

All three humans peel themselves off the earth, and only Gretha bothers to brush away the bits of twigs and leaves that cling. Brida's sleep has made her mellow. Her arms move like flapping silk as she gouges out a rotten log in search of earwigs and beetle larvae, then heats a rock in the fire. After the creepy crawlies have been roasted on it and eaten, she tells the children about a group of rich travellers she'd once seen stop at the Gutendorf tavern. Brida had been sitting at the tavern's long trestle table absorbing a slab of bread and cheese, the value of which would be deducted from what the brewster paid her for her goods. Horses came – it sounded like at least six – and two noblemen, a lady, and her serving woman ducked through the low door, peering around like moles as their pupils adjusted to the dim, smoky room. The lady and one of the men had the same low brow and pigmentless hair and lashes. They wanted to know where they could get a feed for their mounts.

Brida describes how the travellers had stayed standing while they downed their ale. She describes the gold threadwork on the edges of the men's tunics and the whiteness of the lady's hands. She describes their falcons: that the birds' hoods had been made of coloured leather, and that there was a peregrine for the lady, a saker for the man who looked like her, and a lanner for the other. She describes the pearl-headed pins holding the lady's fillet in place and the engraved sapphire bulging like a quail egg from the neck chain of the darker man. As Brida talks, she prods steadily at the floor of the cave with a stick – and not for one moment does she recognise how much her action is like something Hans might do.

There is something Brida has left out of her telling though. When the lady had drifted towards the fire and pushed back the hood of her cloak, she'd dislodged an ivory comb from her hair. It had tumbled down the folds of the cloak and skidded towards Brida's toes, and no one else had seen it happen. Brida's mind had blossomed white hot – then she'd let a corner of her cheese drop below the table. Just as she'd hoped, the two schnauzers lying under the table's far end had leapt to their feet and come sniffing about. They stayed precisely long enough to block any view of Brida's hand reaching down and closing around the comb.

Outside the cave, evening shadows swallow the clearing. A sundew growing in the squelchy soil by the ponds curves its tentacles around a gnat it has trapped, nudging the insect into better contact with the beads of digestive enzyme that the plant has immediately begun to exude. The children and the woman take turns with the axe at chipping up an oak branch to steep for its tannins, then they all sleep.

The night is the warmest one yet. Brida is woken again by the danger calls of birds, and she steps out into a moonless blackness so star spangled that it is dropping silver paint onto a retreating fox's back. She crosses to the snare the animal was headed away from and sees the dark shape of a body in it.

I love you, I love you, I love you, thinks Brida as she eases the noose off the hare's ankle. She spreads the creature out to inspect its long, pale-furred belly and runs her hand over it. *Everything is much better because of you*, she thinks at the corpse, and they are as soft as each other in the kind night.

✕   ✕   ✕

Third chopping. She stands by the falls. She has breakfasted on hare's heart, hare's liver and hare's kidneys. Her blood is whizzing the newly acquired copper, iron and B vitamins around her body to where each is most needed, and her cheeks are pink with optimism as she swings her axe one, two, three times. The sycamore she is chopping into is its own Yggdrasil: the centre of life for innumerable beings – from the millions of aphids suckling on its five-fingered leaves to the symbiotic fungus living inside its root tissues. The children are back at the cave, keeping the flies off the hare's meat and replenishing the water in a pot holding its simmering head and bones. This sycamore is not the tree that Hans wants Brida to cut.

The columns of the forest rise at her back. She pauses for breath and finds herself existing within the force and vasculature of the water that laces her terrain. 'Smack, smack,' says her axe, its impact singing up through the tree into a branch that has died after being girdled of its bark by starving squirrels. The branch crashes to the ground, and Brida leaps aside and straight into Hans, who is coming helter-skelter through the vegetation to find her.

Hans, you flutter your fists excitedly as you gaze past Brida's elbow and tell her why the other tree is the best one to cut. 'You have to come this way,' you say, and when she bends into the sea of blue periwinkles to pick up the axe, off you start to lead the way. But then you don't hear her feet behind you, so you come back and say it again and make your beckoning hand. 'Go back to your sister,' she grunts, and keeps chopping. So you turn and shove your way between the waggling, scratching arms of all the plants that grow between you and your chosen tree, then after you've looked at it you turn and head back to Brida with intolerable agonies in your chest. When you reach her, you scream several times in a way that makes you feel more unified, and you slide yourself in under the leafy part of the big just-fallen branch.

Shortly, Brida will drag this branch to the side – as though there were no one curled beneath it – to get better access to the sycamore's face cut. As you crawl out, *exactly* like a puppy, you will pick up the axe from where she has leant it against the trunk and hurl it out into the middle of the falls.

Part 5

Once Upon a Time

THE STORKS' NEST atop the woodsman's cottage is a hairball coughed up by a troll. It hugs the thatch with a loose cement of sticks, soil and all the accumulated fragments of skin, feather, food and shit that have washed down through the nest's architecture. Its underhang has been excavated, extended and finessed into sub-nests by several pairs of breeding swallows, and at dawn and dusk, they whip in and out of these havens like restless arrows, taking turns to comb insects from the air above the river.

Since their reunion, the storks have mated ten or more times a day. After each coupling, they preen each other's head and neck feathers tenderly and lengthily. A microscopic fungus grows on their feathers – consuming keratin and oil, being consumed in turn by several species of mites.

That's enough mating now, think the storks after twelve days, and they turn their energies towards improving the nest. They start leaving it more often to sift the waterways for tucker. On the sixteenth day, the female lays the third of three chalky white eggs.

I love you, I love you, I love you, she thinks, feeling her belly plumage settle over the full clutch for the first time.

Most everything that lays eggs has done so by now, from skink to cuckoo to leopard slug to nightjar. In the clearing by Brida's cave, the small copper butterflies are working towards their third laying of the season. The males are staking out patches of sunshine in which to pursue and fertilise females, and they will defend these territories like tiny Vikings – chasing off rival males, other insects, even bird shadows. For most larger creatures, the blazing metabolic effort of producing such a proteinaceous packet of genetic material as an egg is not to be repeated lightly. A failed or pilfered clutch will be replaced only if the mother's body can afford it.

Hille's body hasn't produced eggs in four years now. She's eating more with the children gone, but it's too little, too late. Her heart has atrophied beyond repair, all the delivery trucks inside her are empty or have broken down, and nothing arrives where it is needed anymore. Here she is, panting and reeling her way between two rows of skinny leeks, wondering whether hardships are more typically sent by God as punishments or as tests – and whether there is a way to tell one from the other. And now here she is, heading back towards the cottage, now staggering, dropping her armful of vegetables because her vital systems are all folding up like paper fans at the end of a masquerade ball.

She dies just as the male stork arrives back at the nest with a good feed of brook lamprey in his belly. His neck ruff has grown quite shabby now that the breeding season is over.

In the river, an otter couple are mating amidst the fizzing bubbles. In the millpond, the nymph of a blue hawker dragonfly is hunting toad tadpoles. The nymph hatched three full years ago, and soon it will change from a thing that propels itself through the shallows by expelling water from its rectum, into a thing that can fly. It will crawl out of its aquatic crèche and pump air into its body until it splits its skin like the Incredible Hulk splitting his shirt sleeves, then it will pump fluids into its folded wings until they inflate into glassy panes.

Or not. The nymph might be unlucky, as Hille has been. Perhaps its bad luck will take the form of a hungry three-spined stickleback fish, dozens of whom are currently incubating their eggs in mounds of debris on the pond's floor. The male sticklebacks have built these mounds with tunnels running through them to house the eggs, and they swim in place at the tunnels' entrances day and night, fanning oxygenated water into them with their fins. When the eggs start to grow frisky, bumping around with the enthusiasm of the tiny lives forming within them, their fathers increase the ventilation by poking holes into the tunnels.

'Why did we do it if you were going to die anyway?' is not something Craft asks as he sinks to his knees by Hille's spread-eagled figure and begins to sob. Recently, he has started to understand that savagery abounds in the fall of things; he has no blame for anyone.

The female stork flies over him as she leaves for the millpond – it's her turn to go feed now. Her physiology and Craft's are different enough that she doesn't recognise his grieving as what she'd felt when her first mate was killed by a teenager with a bow.

'Idiot!' the young man's family had said when he'd brought the dead bird home. 'Storks kill snakes, and other troublesome creatures too.'

And as though to prove them right, the female stork now scarfs down not one, not two, but three grass snakes – before rounding off her meal with seven doting stickleback daddies.

Ducks, Swan

Once upon a time, it has been four days since Hans threw the axe into the water. Brida and Gretha have spent the first of these labouring along the rocky chaos that flanks the falls, finding places where they could wedge their feet in amidst roots and stones firmly enough to dredge the water's edges with great twiggy branches. The drag on the branches had constantly threatened to pull them off balance, and at one point Brida gripped handfuls of the back of Gretha's apron to brace the girl as she poked at a promising protrusion with a stick. Gretha had been reminded of when she was very small and the cow had been having difficulty giving birth; Hille pulling on the calf's wet ankles with all her might while Craft anchored his feet against the slipperiness of the cow's liquids on the barn floor and pulled on Hille's waist. A late snow had been falling outside.

Hans has spent two nights and a day imprisoned in the mallards' alcove.

'You can't keep him shut up for so long,' Gretha had protested, because her parents have never kept him under the table for this much time.

Brida had been taken aback by the fervency of the girl's distress, and she'd rolled the rock aside. When Gretha had crawled into the alcove and put her hand on her brother, he'd flapped his hands weakly but had kept staring into some inverted middle distance. He'd only done one poo in there that the girl could discover amidst the bracken and the duck shit – and it had been tiny because Brida has continued to always hand him the bowl with the thinnest serving of stew.

Imagine now a warm, soft wind, like the brush of fur on skin. It feels its way over Hans' face as he finally emerges into the clearing, still mute and glassy-eyed. He tucks himself in amongst some rocks and doesn't see his sister aim the slingshot at a red-backed shrike. The bird – who is busy skewering a mayfly it has just caught onto the hawthorn bush it uses as its larder – flaps convulsively to the ground.

Brida does see, and she smiles.

Gretha has also found two squashed mice and a wren in her deadfall traps, but with Brida's grain all but gone and the turnips not yet grown, it's still far from enough – no matter how much they pad the pot with bear's leek and acorn flour. There are eighteen grams of meat on the shrike.

It starts to drizzle. Brida is talking to Gretha of taking her and Hans to Gutendorf when she goes: maybe from there they can find a cart willing to take them on the first leg of the long, hopscotching journey to SMV. The fine droplets stipple Hans' cherub skin, gradually calling him up out of the spectre he has replaced himself with. In the cave that evening he pats his thighs hard all over, up and down, like a never-ending drum solo, and when he starts on his chest and face too, Brida hisses softly through her teeth and hauls him shouting back into the alcove.

'He can come out in the morning,' she says to Gretha as an afterthought, and Gretha nods her assent.

A full moon rules the night. Nervous systems blink on and off like the eyes of dragons. Brida dreams of pebbles that turn into pigs and pigs that turn into huge pitchers of milk. She's at the market in the town near SMV – the one where Orban had once been apprenticed to his cousin the weaver. One of the stalls, which is selling brass cooking pots for a pittance, is staffed by trees. Brida notices that some of these trees have dark streaks of rot in their heartwood and so doesn't buy anything.

Hans dreams of Brida, and she is not even one scrap a person but instead the head and neck of a swan with no body attached. She is flying silently through the forest, which is silent with her.

Crack

DOWN THE SLOPE starts Hans, and his head is chrome and his hands are anodised electric blue. Gretha has clambered onto Brida's shoulders so as to tie the uppermost corners of a bird net to a branch. Her young arms are reaching up to make the last loop when she hears Hans talking himself through the undergrowth. She picks him out from above; she recognises by his gait the intention to move far and fast.

The net, made by Gretha under Brida's instruction – and out of strands from her own long, pale-yellow plaits – has been four days in the making. It is too precious to have its handling rushed. A six-eyed spider crawls back under a shard of bark as the girl's fingers fumble a final knot into existence beside it, then down Brida's tall back Gretha slides, their woollen kirtles dragging against each other as though reluctant to end the meeting. Setting off after her brother, Gretha throws a glance over her shoulder to admire how invisible the net is against the white sky.

Brida's body feels soft and weak everywhere the child's has pressed against it.

Down, down goes Hans, and there is no clear way here because Brida has been careful not to make one. Brambles grab at his calves and write braille books on them in blood; leeches drop onto his feet and release anaesthetic as they latch on. Hans moves towards the most uncluttered place he can see, and he winds up on a ledge jutting above a steep tumble of boulders and blocks. There is no checking his momentum when he feels this way, and he crawls straight over the edge and stretches his toes towards the domed tip of the rock below. He lets himself drop. The granular surface doesn't hold him when he lands, and he flies down the rock's rough shoulder then slams into the floor of a deep cleft.

A full drum kit is playing inside him now, heavy on the cymbals. *I'm not ready to stop*, he thinks, and feels some other iteration of his body climb back up the stone. But his small, grazed limbs refuse to become those of the imagined body – which is mostly that of Gretha, who he's seen pick her way up rock faces before. He knows that her fingertips flare white as they hook themselves over juttings and into micro-crevices, so he pushes his own fingertips against the rock until they blanch – but nothing more happens. 'Out!' he roars, and then again, and so loudly that he has to put his hands over his ears to block out the noise.

On his hundredth time saying it, he looks up and sees his sister's arm hung down the side of the rock towards him, its fingers wriggling like worms on a hook. This looks utterly revolting to him, and he turns his thin frame sideways and shoves it into an impossible crack.

In a not-so-distant ravine, a family of grey wolves lies sprawled beneath an overhang, paws flicking as they dream of running. In his own rocky womb, Hans pushes further into the crack with his bent elbow and knee and discovers that he likes the cold ceramic smell in there. He wants to get the other side of his body in as well, but he's already in as far as he can go. He twists his thigh a little and likes how well he can feel its shape, sandwiched as it is between the two cool, rippled slabs. He can feel the ball of his elbow bone too, and he rotates his wrist to make that ball move so that he can better decipher its bulges. These are marvellous discoveries, but eventually Hans notices the sound of his sister's voice calling his name and decides to go to it.

His elbow refuses to come with him.

He budges it up and down inside the crack, but it's stuck hard. He begins hollering.

'Bump, bump,' goes Gretha's heart as she jogs back into the clearing in search of Brida, but she's nowhere to be found. The girl visits all of the woman's regular foraging spots, eventually finding her in the lee of a high, gorse-clad outcrop. Bees with pollen-heavy thighs drone about the gorse blossom as it sweats its coconut fragrance into the lukewarm sky. Brida has blacked out and is woozily pushing herself up from the ground as Gretha appears through the stunted shrubs.

'Hans is stuck down between some rocks; I think we can only get him out with a rope,' says the girl, watching bits of mica twinkle on the woman's palms as she turns them over to brush them off.

Brida's heavily clouded eyes swing out to the horizon in a disinterested squint.

'I'm too tired now,' she says as she starts off down the ridge, and her walk is like that of a coffin bearer. Not because there is anything sombre in her posture, but because like a coffin bearer, she walks drawn up towards the sky as though carrying something that might belong there.

By the time Gretha gets back to him, Hans' rock well has been swallowed by frigid shadow. She has brought along a ragged pancake made with nettles and birch bark flour, thinking to climb down and feed it to him – but quickly realises that even if she can get down, she'll never get up again with so little light to show her the way. She sings him a song he likes (it's about a hunter who gets eaten by his own dogs as retribution for never giving them enough of the kill), then she tells him that Brida will come in the morning with her rope and her very strong arms and they will get him out. She's optimistic that this is true – though Brida has continued, dazed and aloof, since her faint.

Gretha can see Hans' upturned eyes swimming in his dimly sketched face, and they're like just two more tiny puddles sitting in depressions in the rock. They reflect the darkening sky, and then the emerging stars, but although they dart regularly to-and-fro, only twice does Gretha see them ping towards her face – and

they linger there no longer than on any other point. She sings
him another song (this one is about planting peas), then heads
back to the cave to sleep in the warmth.

The forest has quietened its breathing for the night and is sip-
ping at oxygen, just like its animal inhabitants. In the daylight
of that far-away tropical land where volcanoes – dead, undead,
and oh-so-alive – teem with rainbow-coloured beings, the forest
is awake and inhaling carbon dioxide as it photosynthesises. In
the gigantic storks' nest on the roof of Craft's cottage, the male
stork is dreaming of the water flowing in and around his bill as he
sweeps it side to side across the silty shallows of an endless wetland. He can see with his bill as well as he can with his eyes, and
through the drifting particulates that paint the water with tiger
stripes of darkness and light, he spies his eggs, which are trying
– to his consternation – to hatch early. He wades towards them,
thinking to roll them onto one of the islands of floating debris.
But he's too late; the eggs fall open as he reaches them, and the
babies swim out. And although he's delighted to see them kick
their way childishly towards the surface, he's astonished to realise
that they're not stork babies, but human ones.

Hans

Just before sun-up, Hans yanks his arm out of the crack, breaking the opposite wrist as he topples back onto it. His liberated elbow is studded with crumbs of rock and runnelled with pink gouges, and it quickly swells into a yellow puffball. He doesn't scream but moans – a sound in no way audible from the cave. Yet all the same, Gretha wakes and pushes herself up onto her elbow as though listening.

'We have to get Hans, Brida,' she says to the body stretched out beside her in the dark, and the body's long eyelids winch themselves slowly open.

'You'll have an easier time in finding transport from Gutendorf without him,' mumbles Brida, 'and he'll give us much trouble on our walk to get there.' Her breath is foul with hunger, and her groggy tongue seems offended by the effort of speech.

'You would give him to the forest?' asks Gretha, feeling her skin gather abruptly into goosebumps.

'I would,' says Brida flatly – and the goosebumps dissolve into a cold, dank mist that numbs Gretha's flesh as she gets to her feet.

Outside the cave, birds have begun to twitter. The chinks in the woven door are leaking watery golden light onto the rush mats, and the first mallard is swaggering out of the alcove in anticipation of being let out.

'But his weight on the rope will be too much for me alone,' attempts Gretha as Brida rises gauntly and begins kicking their week-old bedding into a heap to be hauled out and replaced.

'You'd do better to leave him put,' the woman snaps.

Gretha drags the door aside and wanders uncertainly across the clearing. She hesitates by the birch grove, then down, down she goes. Back in the cave, Brida is reaching into the alcove and lifting out the two eggs she finds there. For the first time since the children's arrival, she eats both of them herself. She goes to the drinking-water pond and moves the bramble barrier to the side. Instead of filling a basin and carrying it up the bank as she would usually do, she laves the water directly onto her face and into her mouth, sluicing her gums until the mineral chilliness of it locates her in herself again – much as she'd done when she'd found this clearing after leaving SMV. Much, also, as she and her brother Arnest had done so many years ago when they'd discovered this place together. Replacing the bramble barrier around the pond, Brida recalls making the mittens she'd needed for gathering the brambles: she'd laid the pigman's tunic out flat to judge how much fabric she might steal from its hem, and had seen quite how large it was for his small frame. She'd wondered if it might have come down from an older brother, and if so, whether the pigman's absence billowed hollowly in that brother's days – as Arnest's had in hers after one of their uncles had given him such a knock on the ear that he'd gone to bed and never gotten up again.

The idea that Hans could be missed as a brother doesn't even enter her head, so impossible does it seem to her.

All around Brida, there are creatures caring for other creatures. In a nest amidst the briars, the mate of the red-backed shrike that Gretha killed yesterday is feeding its chicks, feeling horribly stressed by having lost its partner. In the old, uncoppiced woods on the far side of SMV, a pine tree is sending a chemical message through its roots to the *Laccaria* fungus it is partnered with. 'I'm not getting enough nitrogen lately,' it says, and the fungus releases toxins into the soil to kill some springtails, knowing that their bodies will provide nitrogen for the pine as they decompose. Beneath a pollarded oak by the church, an adventuring human baby has crawled onto a cluster of caterpillars that have dropped from the tree. They are the larvae of the oak processionary moth, and their venomous hairs have provoked a severe rash on the baby's arms, sending its worried cousin sprinting to the well with the wailing babe bouncing in her grip.

There is a fraction of Brida that is now occupied by care for Gretha, but the greater part of her is swiftly reverting to her long-held solitary form – as if the children's coming to the cave might be no more than a dream generated during an afternoon nap. As she sits sharpening the pigman's knife on a horsehide strop, she's thinking not about where Gretha might have gone or about Hans being trapped, but about the journey to Gutendorf, which she's never made in as weak a condition as this before. She figures that if she can just catch one fair-sized animal to get her there, she'll be able to join the seasonal work without becoming one of those who collapses in the fields while waiting for the noonday bread.

And Gretha? She has discovered her brother curled awkwardly on the floor of the rock well and has called down to him until he has rolled his head to face her. He is as pale as a cloud – or rather, as an iceberg, what with that blue tinge about his margins. But his eyes hit hers and stick there for a moment, and she tells him to keep watching his rock-framed patch of sky, because she's going to their cottage to fetch help and will send a stork back to wave to him once she gets there. Then she sets off.

Gretha

G RETHA HAS SPENT the whole day bashing along the watercourse of which the falls are a part. This great utterance of water that braids and splits, topples and spits, and eventually arranges itself into the river that glides past the woodsman's cottage and on into SMV, is flowing at speeds of ten to twenty kilometres an hour: comfortably powerful enough to move a two-metre-wide boulder in its path, and certainly powerful enough to knock down a famished eight-year-old girl. That girl has begun a dozen tentative crossings, numbing her hide in the icy water, scanning for protruding branches and rocks that she could grab onto to stop herself from being swept away. But the water is a battering ram and the rocks as slippery as the inside of a cheek, and each attempt has seen her turn back having hardly begun.

Imagine her now sitting at the base of an elderberry tree. She's watching two robins engaged in a furious territory battle. The territory in question is as big as Notre Dame Cathedral and contains many resources worth fighting for. The birds roll on the ground, aiming savage pecks at each other's heads. They splay their wings for support and it makes them look like tiny fan-dancers. Once the intruder is bleeding from his ears and can no longer stand on one of his legs, the defendant doesn't waste any more energy on him.

What a fine elder, the girl thinks, gazing up at the tree's low dome of flower panicles, each white cluster humming with hoverflies, droneflies, ants. She guesses that Brida must come here in summer to pick the fat tassels of berries that will soon start to form. On the far side of the tree a jay has spread itself, wings outstretched, over an ant mound. The outraged ants will spray formic acid into the smothering plumage, killing off many of the bird's bothersome parasites. The child turns back to the water, wanting to try a different route across this broad, shallow stretch – but the sun is dropping, and she knows she needs to get warm and dry before the temperature falls any further.

In sidles the night. Two long-eared owls are perched on the rim of an abandoned crows' nest, grooming themselves, waiting for full blackness to arrive so that they can hunt.

Rope

'Buzz, buzz,' go the bees, bobbing in attentive loops around the first of the foxglove flower spikes to unpurse their purple lips.

Inside his empty cottage, Craft is shifting his gaze from one surface to another, feeling unsure about everything. Outside this storyteller's window, wattles dressed in golden pom-poms puff their honey into the air currents, and currawongs hurl waterfall cries down from the highest eucalypts. And because she wants the sureness of these things, this storyteller pauses and listens and gazes.

Craft comes to his doorway. He pauses and listens and gazes: at the bees, at the foxgloves, at the sky – which is a great pearl today. He thinks about the outside of wood, which is so full of ways of dealing with the world, and he thinks about the inside of wood, and he both loves and trusts it, and hates it for not saving his family.

Some kilometres away, his daughter is about to test her third crossing spot for the morning. She has decided that if she fails here, she'll go back to the cave to see if Brida's mood has changed. Among the rocks by the water's edge, she finds several salmon that a bear has caught and discarded after eating out their brains and internal organs. What a feverishness there is to her movements as she rinses one of the carcasses off and chomps into the tangerine flesh! On her fourth wonderful mouthful, she notices something else wedged between the rocks. It's Brida's axe, of course.

Up, up the slope she goes, encumbered by the salmon she carries in one hand and the axe she carries in the other. She sticks near the water for the sake of not getting lost, and its hundred gushing voices become the voice in which her body speaks with her brain. She follows a tributary by mistake and has to backtrack. She climbs up and down a long welt of rocks until they grow so choppy that it becomes impossible to continue. She loops further away from the water to avoid a group of boar who are merrily grubbing up blue flag iris corms, and then can't find her way back.

When she thinks she might have to spend a second night alone in the forest, she sits down and stares blankly between the trees, letting the mosquitoes settle on her cheeks and hands. They make the most of it for as long as it takes Gretha to heed that preference that living things have for continuing to *try* – even when life is harsh and likely to stay that way.

The wind drops. Without so much swishing, the water becomes audible again. Gretha finds her way back to it and then eventually back to the falls. Above them, a tired blue sky and a transparent gibbous moon. As the girl winds her way towards her brother, she thinks about whether she should bite bites out of the fish and throw them down to him, or throw the whole thing down. Chunks will be easier to chew, but will get covered in grit, which he's funny about on food.

Moss. Hollows. Outstretched roots and fallen logs. Necessity demands that Gretha looks mostly at what's in front of her feet and only occasionally up towards the small patch of treeless sky that she knows marks Hans' location. On the final twist of her ascent, she glances up to check her direction and sees Brida standing on the ledge above the rock well, pulling on a rope. The wind has woken full of renewed gusto after its nap and is sending the woman's short hair out behind her like a flag. Gretha calls Brida's name, but it is whisked from her mouth and blown over her shoulder. She can see the lump of her brother being hauled over the edge now and is about to call out again – when she sees Brida pick up a rock and slam it into the side of Hans' head. The girl's spine jolts. It wants to flick her whole body back and forth like a serpent, but instead she drops it into a crouch amidst the great upturned roots of a fallen beech. Her thumping heart drowns out the sound of a wren's angry cheeps as it hops from root to root, trying to get her attention. The bird's nest-tunnel is in the hardened soil trapped between the roots, and Gretha's shoulder is blocking its entrance. Four species of tiny spiders are brushed onto the girl's hair as she leans into the caked earth.

Slope and beech roots have obscured Gretha's view of the rock ledge itself – so she doesn't see Brida tie Hans' ankles together with a piece of the same cord that already binds his wrists. But then the woman stands up, and Gretha can see her hoisting him over one shoulder and shrugging his inert body into a balanced position. The witch dips one knee to collect her coil of rope and starts off towards the clearing.

Wind

IF THERE ARE, in fact, charioteering gods in the winds, they begin now truly laying the whip to their horses. Saplings are being bent horizontal, and Brida's freckles are being blown across her cheekbones to pile up in drifts by her nose.

At least you will keep the flies away, she nods to the wind.

The woman humps her burden towards the cave, and the girl who has been following her is forced to skirt around the edge of the clearing to avoid being seen. By the time the girl reaches a spot with a good view of the cave's porch, Brida is leaving it. She has shifted Hans to her opposite shoulder and is struggling to keep hold of a large basin with her free hand. She exits the clearing on its far side.

Gretha waits and waits, then pelts across the open space as though the howling sky might tell on her for passing under it. She noses cautiously through the gnashing vegetation, and there is Brida, squatting beneath the same tree they'd hung the hare from last week to let it bleed out – blood they'd caught in the same basin that Brida has just put down.

Brida cannot but think of the pigman as she undresses Hans – the weird mechanics of angling unconscious limbs through openings is too particular not to. But where the pigman had seemed hot pink with energy, Hans is cool, floppy and white. He reminds Brida of nothing so much as a big, dead fish, and if her hands are trembling as she throws her rope over a branch, it's only because she's weak with starvation. She takes her knife from her belt and drops it into the basin.

The wind is flinging Hans' curls across his forehead, and from where she's hiding Gretha can't tell if it's only this that's making his eyelids seem to move. Brida kneels to thread the dangling rope-end through the cord that binds Hans' ankles. At this, Gretha bolts forward and brings the axe down. It glances off the side of Brida's skull and slips down to gash the back of her ear before lodging itself in her shoulder.

Claws crawl across the ground towards her. Her ear is sending streams of blood down the gullies of her long neck, and her collarbone is fractured. She can smell pickled herring. She attempts to lift her hand to her head but discovers that her arm won't work.

Brida, there's something being pulled out of your neck from behind, tugging you backwards – then an almighty crack on the childlike curve of your occipital lobe.

×　×　×

In the first instant of dying, Brida's vision becomes crisper than it's been in years. As one wind god triumphs momentarily over the others, she can see every leaf in the forest pointing in the same direction.

In the second instant of dying, her eye sockets feel to be made of something very thin and cold. She thinks it might be white quartz, or eggshells blown of their contents.

In the final instant, there's just the leaves again, inside and out.

Gretha's blood is a tsunami. She tries to untie Hans' ankles, but no matter how much her fingers fumble at the knots she can't make any progress. She's jerking between the two bodies, hoping neither is dead, but finally coordinates her marionette limbs enough to drag the rope down from the branch and wind it around Brida's wrists – just in case. Brida has collapsed onto her side, and the elegant line of her kicked-out legs and the curve of her haunch remind this storyteller of a leaping deer.

Gretha checks for and finds warm breath coming from her brother's nostrils, and a thick harp string is plucked inside her and vibrates throughout her central matter. Realising that Hans will need to eat when he wakes up, she starts off towards where she abandoned the salmon, all the way back at her hiding spot within the fallen beech's roots. But she's terrified to leave the two bodies, and twice she doubles back to check on them before running the whole way to the fish. The headless salmon is absolutely covered with ants, and when Gretha hooks her fingers into its stomach cavity, they stream up her arm as she runs the journey in reverse. As she passes the hair net she'd been so proud of, she notices that there's a linnet caught in it, gone limp with the exhaustion of trying to free itself.

The bodies are as she left them. She collects coals from the hearth inside the cave then arranges kindling near Hans' motionless feet. She starts to cry, then to sob so hard that she can't see what she's doing. The wind is squalling almost fiercely enough to dry her tears as fast as they come – but not quite.

Gretha knows now that Brida is dead.

Imagine the girl's shaky hands as she arranges branches into a windbreak, then gets enough flames going to singe some shreds of salmon. The smell of it drags Hans from his concussion – though his eyes still want to close much more than they want to open. He retches yellow juice when she tries to push chewed-up fish into his mouth with her thumb, but swallows eagerly when she tips a thin ribbon of water between his lips. Knowing that she won't be able to move him without his cooperation, she goes to the cave for blankets. Then, as the sun entirely leaves their side of the earth, she curls around her brother, and the furious, buffeting wind takes over the job of defining the world.

Fox

THE STORKS WAKE during the night to nudge their eggs around. They check the temperature of each and adjust its position accordingly. The roaring wind is kicking their small head-feathers up into a cancan, and the male snugs his beak deeper into his breast as he hears the distant crack of a massive limb being wrenched from the linden tree in the centre of SMV. In the wall below the nest, the door to the cottage bangs open, but Craft doesn't bother to get up and shut it.

At Hans' feet, the embers of Gretha's fire pulse orange then black as the weather goes at them like a bellows. A spark is lifted into the darkness, pirouettes, then drops onto Brida's hair. It begins to frizzle the strands into a miniature version of those grassfires that the storks seek out in Africa. While the burn dies out at her scalp, the tiny, stinking fragments of burnt hair float up into the argumentative currents. Most will descend again to land on the surfaces of the surrounding forest, but a few will travel higher. One or two may even make it high enough to join those particles of volcanic ash that are still wandering about the stratosphere.

In a moment, Hans will sit up. His re-entry into the world will be like a birth, so overwhelming will it be to swim into a consciousness that includes the pain of his wrist and elbow, the wind, the full moon briefly doubled before his eyes. 'Kartin!' he will whimper, hearing the black mare's hoofbeat in the thudding of his eardrums.

Gretha will wake beside him and get them both into the cave. When she comes back at first light for the knife, she'll see a fox vixen with four half-grown kits feasting on Brida's blistered and bloody head. The hungry creatures will trot off into one of their corridors through the bracken at the girl's approach.

Gretha will say a prayer for Brida's soul, then she'll go back to the cave to cook fish for breakfast. The wind will be dead in the grey sky.

Pollen

ONCE UPON A time, two children move slowly through the forest, because Hans is still unsteady on his feet. The gale has brought down many trees and even more branches, and the walk to the falls looks so altered that the children veer off course and have to wander the slope looking for a landmark. A misting drizzle starts up, and Gretha's heart sinks to note how much the quickly slickening surfaces further retard their pace. She takes the basket off her back and puts some pieces of birch bark over the parcels inside it to keep them dry. There is the last of Brida's stores of barley, beech nuts and acorn flour. Also, four hard-boiled duck eggs, and a gluey patty of flour boiled up with the salmon scraps and some new dandelion leaves. Beneath these edible treasures sits Brida's rope – amongst other things. And what of Hans' fractured wrist? Gretha has bound it in imitation of what she's seen done on a calf. She has also salved his wounded elbow with the waxy stuff that she'd seen

Brida use on burns. While searching for this ointment, she had discovered the ivory comb.

Hans is talking a lot, peppering the dull air with anxious questions about where they're going, how they'll get across the falls, and where Brida is.

'You're not strong enough to chop the tree for the bridge,' he states, and Gretha reminds him that the axe is lost in the water anyway.

She is relieved to watch him search his memory and find nothing there to contradict her with.

The girl's head is taut with thoughts of a spot downstream where she'd tried to cross on her attempted journey home: a set of barrelling rapids with a dead elm fallen partway across them from the far side. She imagines lassoing one of its branches and wading through the frenzied water with Hans on her back, his bruised and weeping elbow hooked around her throat, crushing her windpipe as it always does when she piggybacks him. She imagines the awful action of the current on his broken wrist as they cross the deeper channel that runs next to the bank. She imagines getting him to sing as they cross, and starts inventing a rhyme that might focus his attention on something other than terror.

When they reach the falls, relief rushes up and hits her in the face like a cold wave. There is a new tree bridging the water.

As much as this storyteller might like it to be, it is not the tree that Hans had decided they should cut, but the sycamore that Brida had been chopping down when Hans had thrown her axe into the water. The children inch across its rough length, Hans shaking visibly with the concentration of working his way around the branches with only one hand at his disposal. When they reach the far side, he stays silent as they push through and out of the sycamore's canopy, then stream into the forest like two figments of its imagination.

A pale lemon sunshine replaces the drizzle. Spruce pollen is released in great plumes and moves through the trees like a ghost looking for love. The female stork has spiralled up from the nest and is soaring far above the forest on her way to a frog-rich marsh – but even from this height she can see the drifts of yellow rolling across the treetops, forming a pastel skin on every lake and pond it blows over. When the children stop to share their fish patty, they first hold clusters of male spruce cones above it, tapping the pollen out of them until the nutty powder coats their lunch like jaundiced icing sugar. Then it's back to sploshing through streams and huffing up ridges, always following the bleached disc of the sun through the flickering branches.

At one point, Gretha spots a long sweep of quaking aspen that she remembers passing on their journey into the forest. The introduction of hope is disarming. Pulled by the part of her that is most like Hans, she steers them into the grove, craving the gorgeous white noise of the aspens' leaves rustling in the breeze. These leaves have flattened petioles that cause them to twist and shiver against each other in the slightest movement of air. Five hundred years after the time of this story, a similar rustling will draw a man across a tobacco field in the newly formed state of

Ohio, USA to stand by a shelterbelt of cottonwood trees – who share a petiole-structure with their aspen cousins.

The canopy closes, the canopy dilates, contracts, opens. A small meadow framing a gargantuan fallen oak is throbbing with bearded iris, their two-toned blue perfectly mirroring the high and low reaches of the intensifying sky. The land becomes less folded, the forest floor more obviously laced with deer trails. A small piece of white quartz is glaring incongruously from atop the green velvet of a fat mossy root – but the children walk right past it, distracted by a noise that might be wild boar, or might just be pigs from SMV turned loose into the forest now that winter is over. Wasps sniff out the raw flesh of Hans' elbow and surround it with a small hovering constellation that he's moving too slowly to lose. When Gretha rips off his torn-up sleeve and uses it to cover the wounds, he's as chuffed by the air flowing past his one naked armpit as he had been panicked by the wasps.

They pass within fifty paces of the holly with the doughnut of hidden space beneath its boughs, and something in the trigonometry of branch to trunk to earth has started to hum familiarly. They pause to eat the boiled duck eggs, and the big stone they sit on siphons the warmth out of their thighs and redistributes it to the nine-hundred-year-old lichens that mottle its surface.

Not far away lie the remains of the red deer carcass that had nurtured so many bluebottle maggots. It's mostly bones and a bustling society of microarthropods now, ringed by a floral border of everything that has germinated from the droppings of the birds who'd come to eat the maggots. Those maggots that escaped being eaten have pupated into iridescent blue flies, a few of whom have moved deeper into the forest and are right now feeding and laying eggs in what's left of Brida's head. Others are bothering the inner corner of Gretha's eyes. She swats them away as the river – broad and flat now – appears between the trees.

River

ONCE UPON A time, Hans and Gretha approach that water that all the terrain at their backs has gathered into this shining, sliding sheet. On its far side, they can see meadows into which they have cantered Craft's mare, chased escaped goats and brought the cow to graze. Without warning, Hans wades into the smooth, muscular water towards that known place of swaying grass – and is picked up and carried away, his damaged arms useless against the river's sure, strong grasp.

An otter stands on the far bank crunching on a freshwater crayfish as Gretha sloshes in and releases herself to the current. Her basket bobs up behind her, then slowly fills with water. 'Blub, blub,' go the air pockets in the parcels of beechnuts and barley, and they float out of the tilted opening. The otter sees the odd objects spinning in an eddy and slips into the water to investigate. Gretha watches Hans' skeletal head sailing briskly along ahead of her like a downy feather fallen from a passing stork's breast. She scrabbles the basket from her back, but before releasing it pulls the comb – which is inlaid with gold – from its depths and plunges it into the dense matrix of hair at the top of one of her braids. She swims better now; gains on Hans, catches hold of his waist and tries, unsuccessfully, to kick them towards the bank. The boy is struggling to keep his head above the surface. He gulps water as the monotonous sound of sheep being moved drifts up the valley from SMV. In just a moment, the riverbed will pinch into the long narrow stretch that is spanned by the bridge near the children's home.

The afternoon is late now and warm. At the Gutendorf tavern, the brewster's rottweiler has moved from its spot by the hearth out into the strip of shade below the eaves. The years of famine have reduced its bulk to a slack bagginess, and the cool of the ground slides into its organs too quickly. It looks accusingly at the low murky horizon, then lays its muzzle along its paws and rotates its ears to better monitor the sounds of the building it has just left.

In his workshop in that city where Rotting Splintering stands, Orban is working at his loom with all the windows thrown open to the light. This light sits in warm rectangles on a recent delivery of yarn, and on the cheekbones of a young man who is inspecting that yarn for defects. The youth is Brida's half-brother, and his cheekbones are Brida's cheekbones, with the same cautious electricity zapping around the eyes above them.

Has it been this warm in the last four years? This storyteller suspects not: on a bend in the river near the woodsman's cottage, a duck is pulling out fluffy chest feathers and laying them over her eggs to protect them from the sun. In the woods at her back, Craft is thinning the regrowth on the ash-tree pollards, his face glistening with sweat. The mother duck looks up from her nest to see Gretha losing hold of Hans as he's swept around the bend and into a floating raft of vegetation trapped against the downstream bank. His lips are wet and white. He tries to clamber onto the tangled mat of broken rushes and knotted weeds, but it folds beneath his weight, so he kicks and claws through it towards the osier willow that crowds the river's edge, grabs a drooping cane, hauls himself along its length until his chin is hooked over the high bank and his small toes are pointed into the silt. Gretha is soon beside him, hanging on to her own cane, garnering strength.

After a while they hoist themselves into the growth that hugs the water, and topple through it to emerge into the burning sunshine.

'Clop, clop,' go Craft's wooden shoes as he runs towards his children across the bridge.

Gretha checks his bobbing eyes and sees shame roiling like lava beneath the astonished blue.

Part 6

Once Upon a Time

ON THE DAY that the third stork egg hatches, the smallest person comes into the yard for the first time since returning to the cottage. One of his wrists is bandaged and his other elbow is a veritable coral reef of encrustations. He walks backwards until he has a good view of the nest, then gazes at it with mirrorballs in his eyes. A while later he flaps his arms a bit, and the storks recognise that he is strengthening his wing muscles.

The morning's quilt of cloud thins into scattered curds, and yet still he stands there – sometimes stepping from side to side, sometimes flapping. Mostly just looking.

'Peck, peck,' goes the chick who is trying to get out of the third and final egg, and its nest mates topple about on their puny pink-grey legs. The pecking has been going on since dusk yesterday, and the chick is quite worn out. The two adult storks move about the nest constantly, prodding the egg gently now and then with their vermillion bills.

The river floods. Because the land had barely dried after the years of rain, the muscles in the brows of the people of SMV pucker with worry and stay that way for weeks. For the storks, however, the shallowly drowned land is a boon – especially now, with chicks to feed. The female hunts an ephemeral pond for minnows, extending a wingtip across the water before retracting it with a sharp flick to scare the fish into action. She catches a gullet-full and brings them home to the chicks, regurgitating them into a shining mound on the nest floor.

The smallest person has taken up climbing the pear tree near the cottage to get a better view of the nest. Sometimes he stays there long after the sun has set, and the middle-sized person comes into the yard and cries out into the dark until the smallest one swivels himself on the branch and climbs cautiously down to the ground.

The barley ripens, the flood waters recede. In the vegetable garden by the cottage beneath the storks' nest, radishes pop out of the ground daily and are taken inside by the middle-sized person. She currently has conjunctivitis, as does the smallest one. The big person is yet to be infected, so the job falls to him of warming water each morning and soaking the two smaller people's eyelids until the gunk gluing them together softens. Atop the roof, the storks are engaged in their own scenes of parental tenderness. In hot weather, they take turns at umbrella duty, maximising the shade their bodies cast by standing over the chicks and inching around the nest as the sun arcs across the sky. They ferry beakfuls of water from the river for the chicks to drink and then ferry more to dribble over their fuzzy heads. What a mewling racket the babies set up when they're hot or hungry! They try to copy their parents' clattering noise too, but their beaks are still pliable brown things, and the sound produced is more soft-shoe shuffle than tap dance.

For the first three weeks of their lives, the youngsters are never left unsupervised. The hazards of their own youthful stupidity aside, the chicks might be attacked by martens, ravens, or even an unmated stork attempting a takeover bid on the nest. The babies' little bodies are working hard to manufacture their denser second layer of woolly down, and their hunger cries see their parents stretch their foraging into the night whenever the skies are clear enough. Each time mother and father trade places, they greet each other with heads thrown back and beaks going like red castanets.

Several women in SMV begin to menstruate again after having stopped during the famine. The stork chicks' bills begin to change colour and harden. On hot afternoons the middle-sized person takes up swimming the black mare into the river to cool them both down, sometimes returning at dusk to wade in the slimy shallows as microbats whizz about her head hoovering up clouds of midges. Even from their nest, the storks can hear the frog chorus change as she pushes her calves idly through the water.

Now the big person is leading a new chestnut cow into the barn end of the cottage. The storks know nothing about money or about the gold and ivory comb the big person has recently sold – but they do know that a scatter of rye kernels escaped from some bulging sackfuls brought in on the mare's back yesterday, and that doves have been pecking about the yard after them.

The father stork disgorges a mess of insects and worms in front of his children, and they dive in to enjoy this best of baby foods. The mother pumps her wings and rises off the side of the nest into the air, her black parts sheening purple-green in the sun like an oil spill. *I'm tired, but strong,* she thinks. She spirals upwards until she can slip into a thermal that will let her glide effortlessly towards a string of ponds six kilometres away. There, she'll wade past beavers harvesting wads of last year's withered sedge to incorporate into their lodges and will catch a succession of narrow young bream for herself. Then, she'll bring a grass snake home for the chicks to play tug-of-war with – until the strongest wins and scarfs down the whole rubbery length of the thing.

A buzzard is circling. The father stork takes in its presence and settles closer to the chicks. The afternoon is a warm bubble, and the smallest person is standing in the shade of the pear tree again, watching the father stork watch the buzzard's shadow move across the bare earth of the yard. The smallest person hums contentedly and listens to the whisking sound of the middle-sized person sweeping the floor rushes out of the cottage. His mind is such that he doesn't think forward to the moment when she'll call him over to help haul the spent rushes onto the vegetable garden. He is aware of the ground rocking sweetly beneath his bare feet, and of the triangle made by the raptor's shadow, the stork's eye and his own eye. Nothing else.

'Flump, flump,' goes the air beneath the mother stork's wings as she arrives and tries to alight on the nest, but the chicks' excitement at her return is so extravagant that they're hobbling around and making it almost impossible to avoid being landed on. She finally manoeuvres her long legs into a gap, greets her partner, and trickles water from her beak over her panting children. In the humid north of the same landmass on which this storyteller will one day live, a black-necked stork returns to his nest and regurgitates a torrent of cooling water mingled with tiny fish all over his hatchlings.

From beneath the old oak log near the cottage, stag beetles emerge from the soil. The pear tree's blossoms have mostly been pollinated and now begin swelling their ovaries into fruit. By this time last year, all four chicks in the storks' clutch were dead after a meal of frogs that had been infected with intestinal trematodes. By this time next year, a poor season will have driven the desperate parent storks to kill and cannibalise their runtiest chick in the hope of leaving enough food to see the stronger ones through. *This* year, all three chicks will survive and, like all young storks, will leave for Africa before their parents do, flying the twenty-thousand-kilometre journey without ever having been shown the way. Tiny black scapulars and flight feathers have already begun to emerge from their shoulders and wings, and the father stork sits snugly beside their trio of heartbeats and allows his eyes to close. He dozes, and drifting through his sensory map of himself is a memory of clacking his beak against his partner's as they copulated again, and again, and again.

The decimated population of SMV begins cutting hay, and the storks follow the harvesters to exploit the exodus of small creatures that the scythes leave in their wake. Towards the end of the harvest, the big person brings a new big person back to the cottage with him, and she stays there, because they both need help to be able to do what life asks of them.

Seven years pass. Imagine the father stork on his southbound migration, and imagine him now being blown off course above the rice fields of Andalusia. He can't find a thermal to carry him back above land, and after hours of gruelling flapping he drops onto the choppy surface of the sea. He's too spent to be able to take off again, and once the harsh brine works its way past his feathers' protective coating they'll become waterlogged, and he'll be dragged under by his sodden wings.

The mother stork will return to the nest and accept a new mate who is many years her junior. Together, they'll produce three eggs but will lose one to an interloper, because the young father is unpractised at defending a clutch. 'Thud, thud,' his heart will go every time another male stork flies over the cottage in the weeks to come.

One day, the new father will be diligently scanning his surrounds from his vantage point in the nest, and he'll see several people who don't live in the cottage approach the building and duck under its lintel. They'll reappear carrying the bodies of the two big people, and also that of the smallest person – the one who stands in the yard and watches the storks' comings and goings. The middle-sized person – who will have become big

herself by then – will follow the strangers out. She'll be dragging
a straw mattress, and the ends of her long yellow braids will
catch pieces of escaped straw that will dangle there and make the
braids look longer still. She'll knot these braids behind her neck,
then ignite the mattress with a burning stick, poking it back and
forth through the flames until there's only cinders left.

The young father stork will take off through the smoke in search
of water ribbons with which to strengthen a weak spot in the nest,
which is already thirty years old. It will stand – and be used – for
another eighty, only collapsing because the cottage's roof does.

Coda

Here is the jungle, and here is a sun skink, basking on the shoulder of a tarmac airstrip. A flock of munia finches tense their minuscule chest muscles as the air above them begins to shudder. 'Watch out!' they cry as they take off, and the skink tilts an eye towards the growing metal dot in the sky. It's an aeroplane, lowering itself through the sepia haze that hangs above the jungle and obscures the upper reaches of the ex-volcano.

Sitting on the plane is a thirty-nine-year-old German woman. She has pale blonde hair and a wary, roundish face. She might or might not be a distant descendent of Gretha's – this storyteller isn't sure.

The woman has come to the archipelago in the hope of being surrounded by species that aren't her own – an experience that has become difficult to find in her homeland, and which feels brittle even when it is found. She knows nothing about the fragments of 1.4-million-year-old giant stork bones that lie buried somewhere on the ex-volcano's flank. Nor does she know about the eruption, or how its ash travelled around the globe.

The plane's wheels hit the ground awkwardly, and the woman peers through the smeary window. She sees welted cracks in the runway where the various plants that were burnt to clear the area are trying to break through so they can get at the light. In the tighter cracks, there are thermophilic bacteria living, multiplying, taking advantage of the heat stored by the black asphalt.

Later, the woman steps out of a mini-van by an area of huge primaeval-looking trees. They are a popular attraction and, feeling a desire to distance herself from this fact, she wanders not into the trees but away from them to stand in a red-earthed clearing on the far side of the parking area. While she waits for her group to disperse down the designated walkways, she looks up at the caldera of the ex-volcano, then past it to the new peak that has sprouted from its shoulder. Her head is exploding, pounding under the steamy green sky as an autoimmune condition prevents her small blood vessels from dilating sufficiently to accommodate the heat. A breeze picks up, and she feels the shadow of a large coconut palm's great rustling leaves shift over her scorching shoulders.

I love you, I love you, I love you, she thinks.

That night she eats rice with a greyish hard-boiled egg, greens that she doesn't know come from a papaya tree, and tiny fried fish of the sort that would slide down a stork's long throat like champagne bubbles. She joins a boat trip to view fireflies, then wishes she hadn't when the man steering the boat mentions how many more of the luminous insects there used to be before the palm oil plantations extended so far into the jungle. These kinds of losses are why she's chosen not to have children.

'Blink, blink,' flash the rear ends of the adult fireflies as they zoom around the riverside vegetation. They produce their pulses of light in a pattern specific to their species so that they can find each other and mate. In hidey-holes in the riverbank, their larvae pulse with a dimmer light, reminding predators of how awful they taste – although an uninitiated frog has just swallowed several of the tiny grubs whole, and their lights are still glowing inside the creature's stomach as it kicks hastily away from the approaching boat. On a nearby arenga palm, a long wound in the bark has attracted fruit flies who are feeding on the fermenting sap. On the far side of the new volcano's flank, a man squats outside the monitoring hut, plucking ticks from the neck fur of a caramel-coloured dog. By a nesting platform in Switzerland, a white stork who has been imported from Algeria as part of a reintroduction program is preening his wing feathers. Now he is leaping into the sky in search of a warm, rising current of air.

Acknowledgements

Thank you to Richard J. Camilleri, for being the person I wanted to write this book for.

Thanks also to Kat Lavers and Frances Rowland for their help with typing, and to Daiv Lown and Catherine O'Caroll for input on matters medical. The Okataina Volcanic Centre in New Zealand were incredibly generous with their time over multiple phone calls, and the Victorian Anglers' Association gave much-appreciated advice on fishing and salmon anatomy.

GSP Personnel

EDITORIAL TEAM

Georgia Cooper – Production Manager

Ozlem Kazanaksu – Submissions Manager

Jonathan Almeida Santos – Commissioning Editor

Rhea Candy – Commissioning Editor

Carissa Chye – Structural Editor & Co-Lead Copyeditor

Hollie Whitlock – Lead Structural Editor & Copyeditor

Dai-An Le – Co-Lead Copyeditor

Rohana Atkinson – Structural Editor & Copyeditor

Claudia Mirabello – Typesetter & Designer

SALES, PUBLICITY & MARKETING TEAM

Maryel Sousa – Sales, Publicity & Marketing Team Lead

Anna-Lyse Fazio – Social Media & Marketing Producer

Ainsley Atinon – Social Media & Website Producer

Chrysilla Angelia Djaja – Sales & Publicity Manager

Valleryna Putri Amanda – Sales & Publicity Manager

GSP Acknowledgements

Thank you to Annie Raser-Rowland for sending us the manuscript of *Once*. We are delighted to be publishing your extraordinary novella. Thank you to Terri-ann White for agreeing to launch it, to IngramSpark for printing and distribution, to Tim Fluence for his design advice and Matt Holden for his technical assistance with the cover.

Thanks to Remi Shapiro-Jones, the student commissioning editor who first read Annie's manuscript for GSP and identified its potential; also, to other members of GSP who have read it since. Thanks to the remarkable group of students at GSP this semester who edited the manuscript; designed, typeset and proofread the book; and worked on the sales and marketing campaign. Last but not least, thanks to the School of Culture and Communication, and its head, Professor Paul Rae, for their continuing support.

Sybil Nolan
Publisher at GSP

www.ingramcontent.com/pod-product-compliance
Lightning Source LLC
Chambersburg PA
CBHW061102100726
47911CB00012B/349